Grimgar of Fantasy

level.13 - Heart, Open, A New Door

Written by: **Ao Jyumonji**
Illustrations by: **Eiri Shirai**

When they passed through the door, there was wind blowing beyond it, and something about the air was plainly different.

**The road
to Alterna**

*Feelings fail to become
words, and vanish into
the night sky.*

Grimgar
of
Fantasy
and
Ash

GRIMGAR OF FANTASY AND ASH, LEVEL. 13

Copyright © 2018 Ao Jyumonji
Illustrations by Eiri Shirai

First published in Japan in 2018 by
OVERLAP Inc., Ltd., Tokyo.
English translation rights arranged with
OVERLAP Inc., Ltd., Tokyo.

Follow Seven Seas Entertainment online at
sevenseasentertainment.com.
Experience J-Novel Club books online at j-novel.club.

TRANSLATION: Sean McCann
J-NOVEL EDITOR: Emily Sorensen
COVER DESIGN: KC Fabellon
INTERIOR LAYOUT & DESIGN: Clay Gardner, George Panella
COPY EDITOR: Brian Kearney
PROOFREADER: Stephanie Cohen
LIGHT NOVEL EDITOR: Nibedita Sen
PREPRESS TECHNICIAN: Rhiannon Rasmussen-Silverstein
PRODUCTION MANAGER: Lissa Pattillo
MANAGING EDITOR: Julie Davis
ASSOCIATE PUBLISHER: Adam Arnold
PUBLISHER: Jason DeAngelis

ISBN: 978-1-64505-300-2
Printed in Canada
First Printing: May 2020
10 9 8 7 6 5 4 3 2 1

Grimgar of Fantasy and Ash

level. 13 — Heart, Open, A New Door

Presented by
AO JYUMONJI

Illustrated by
EIRI SHIRAI

Table of Contents

Grimgar
of
Fantasy and Ash

1 | Dreams, Freedom, and Borders

BENEATH THE SCORCHING HEAT of the sun, the darkly-tanned crew of the ship lowered a ladder down onto the pier.

Ginzy, the captain of the *Mantis-go*, stood on the bridge, looking on arrogantly with his arms crossed.

When Haruhiro waved, Ginzy raised his jaw, making his fish-like face (because what was he if not a fish?) twist.

Was that a smile? Or a smirk, perhaps? It was hard to tell.

The voyage had taken five days, including the day of departure and arrival, but even now, at the end of it, Haruhiro still didn't like that man. Of course, he'd never had any desire to make friends with him in the first place, so he didn't feel particularly disappointed by that.

Despite being captain, Ginzy wasn't just disliked by his crew; they hated him. They seemed to hold him in contempt. He was utterly lacking in personal virtue, and had no manners or charm whatsoever. Why had the K&K Pirate Company made that damn sahuagin the captain of the *Mantis-go*?

Ginzy and the founder of K&K, Kisaragi, were best buds, so it might have been an example of cronyism, so to speak. There was something to be said for not letting personal feelings get too involved in staffing decisions.

Not that it mattered.

...Well, maybe it did.

Anyway, with the ladder before him, Haruhiro looked to the faces of each of his comrades.

Kuzaku was here. Big as always, of course. He wasn't going to be getting any smaller.

Having gone through a bad case of seasickness again, Shihoru looked like she wasn't doing so well. Merry was sticking close by her, a look of concern on her face.

Setora was here, too. The gray nyaa, Kiichi, was with her.

That was all. Yume had decided to stay with Momohina, K&K's KMW, for a while.

Incidentally, that title, KMW, was short for "Kung-fu Mage Woman," or something like that. A little ridiculous, no?

Regardless, because of that, they couldn't cut ties with K&K. Not until Yume came back, at least.

Still, to be honest, it felt off somehow, not having Yume with them.

I want to get stronger, Yume had said.

It wasn't hard to understand that. Haruhiro would like to be stronger, too, if he could. However, Haruhiro had no such hopes for himself, so he tended to focus on raising the overall level of the party. Unlike Haruhiro, Yume probably felt she could still keep going, that there was room for her to improve.

In point of fact, Yume hadn't been using all of her undiscovered potential. Haruhiro agreed she had room to grow. But still... did it have to be now?

She was a hunter, so what was becoming a kung-fulier supposed to do?

Besides, what was a kung-fulier anyway?

Even setting that aside, he'd have liked her to at least talk to him about it first. Either way, if Yume had insisted, Haruhiro might not have stopped her. But shouldn't she have given him time to get ready to accept it? It was a lot to process, you know?

During the rocky voyage, he had contemplated what their battle tactics might look like without Yume, but he couldn't help but feel uneasy. It was huge, the hole she was leaving behind. Unbelievably huge.

Yume wasn't good at thinking things through logically, but she had an animal-like, instinctive sort of perception. Perhaps she'd had a strong sense that her comrades would be in trouble without her, and that was why she hadn't been able to tell them what she wanted to do. But, after agonizing over it for a long time, she'd suddenly made the call. That was very like Yume.

Haruhiro didn't have any intention of blaming her for it, but her absence was, in many ways, really going to hurt. As the leader, he couldn't let that show in front of the rest of their comrades, which made it all the worse.

He wished Yume being gone was just a dream.

Perhaps that sounded like a pun, since her name literally meant "dream," but that was honestly and truly how he felt. They couldn't turn back to the Emerald Archipelago to drag her back now, though, so he was just going to have to accept reality.

Fortunately, Yume would be rejoining the party eventually. She wouldn't break her promise. Haruhiro tended to be a pessimist, but he could take an optimistic view on that one point. He just needed to be patient for half a year, until Yume was back. He just needed to hold out until then. He'd manage, somehow.

...Or so he hoped.

No, no matter what happened, he'd have to manage somehow.

Once he descended the ladder from the ship to the pier, he wasn't exactly sure how, he felt a sudden, drastic change in the atmosphere around him.

"It's probably just in my head..." he murmured, looking around.

Haruhiro looked out over the famous free city of Vele. The pirate town of Roronea had been raucously busy, and even after the dragon attacks, the port had been bustling with many pirate ships. But the scale of Vele was different. It was on a whole other level.

Who knew how many piers the port of Vele had, or how many ships were moored there? There were too many to even begin to count.

There was a vast number of laborers carrying cargo up and down the wharves and piers, an unending number of sailors working on and around their ships, and shouting and laughter carried from every which where.

There were well-dressed men and women riding in litters and rickshaws to be seen here and there, too, but who were they?

Naturally, there were humans like Haruhiro and the party, but there were also burly, green-skinned orcs, too. There were also pointy-eared elves, bearded dwarves built like barrels, undead who looked far too sickly, and goblins and kobolds.

"Hey, that's..." Setora's eyes went wide as she looked at one of the laborers.

At some point, Kiichi had gotten up on Setora's shoulders—no, he had wrapped himself around her neck. He was one gutsy nyaa, but maybe all the noise had gotten to him.

The laborer in question had a great amount of luggage on his back. However, that back was the lower half of him. In other words, it wasn't his back at all. The man, incredibly, had four legs. The upper half was human, but the lower half was equine. He even had a tail.

"A centaur," Merry whispered.

"Ohh, so that's one..." Haruhiro answered.

He had heard of them before. The half-human, half-horse centaurs. If he was recalling correctly, they might be residents of the Quickwind Plains. This might be the first time he'd seen one.

"The guy's big. I bet he's got some serious horsepower." Kuzaku grinned. "You know, because he's a horse?"

"Not funny." Setora rejected the joke.

Kuzaku arched his eyebrows as if hurt. "No way. That one was no good?"

"Your sense of humor lacks any taste whatsoever."

"Nah. That's rich coming from you, Setora-san."

"What is that supposed to mean?" she asked indignantly.

As they emerged from the port, the city of Vele quickly began to give off an air of elegance.

The buildings of Alterna were what one might call simple and rugged, if one was feeling kind; they were just solid, not fashionable. Wood or stone, the buildings were left the color of whatever they were built with.

But in Vele, white walls were the default, and the roofs were brilliant colors. There were many sculpted pillars and doors, and even the windows and door frames had some small amount of molding. Glass windows weren't uncommon, either.

Maybe it was because they were walking down the main street, but there were an awful lot of people and carts traveling back and forth.

"Man, Vele's so urban," Kuzaku said with a sigh in the middle of all the noise.

"Eek...!" Shihoru was nearly bowled over by a passerby.

Kuzaku went, "Hey, wait!" and tried to object.

The guy stopped and turned around. His neck and arms were so thick, you had to laugh, and his shoulders were built up to the point it was ridiculous. He even looked taller than the already-tall Kuzaku.

He sure is green, Haruhiro thought.

He just couldn't get used to seeing that green skin. No matter how you looked at him, the guy was an orc.

"Wazza. Danaggwa!" the passing orc shouted.

"...No. I don't understand what you're saying, okay?"

Kuzaku was picking a fight with the passing orc. Surprisingly, he could be really aggressive about things like this.

Haruhiro placed a subtle hand on Kuzaku's hip. "What're you picking a fight for? Apologize."

"But this ass, you saw what he did to Shihoru."

"Um... Kuzaku-kun." Shihoru tried to smile while Merry supported her. "It's because I wasn't watching where I was going well enough..."

"Well, if that's what you say, then fine..." Kuzaku muttered.

"Ganna! Nndegan!" Spittle flew from the passing orc's mouth as he closed in on Kuzaku.

"No, listen!" Having gotten a face full of spit, Kuzaku snapped. "I told you, I don't understand! How about speaking a language I know, huh?!"

"Screw! You!"

"Whoa, buddy, I think you're looking for trouble, huh?!" Kuzaku yelled. "I'll sell you some at a discount!"

"Whoa! I said, cut it out!" Haruhiro quickly got between the passing orc and Kuzaku. He didn't know orcish, but when he desperately explained the situation, along with some pantomime, the passing orc left easily enough, which was a relief.

That said, they hadn't started to attract a crowd, which meant incidents like this had to be a daily occurrence in Vele, so maybe the orc hadn't been that angry, either.

"Don't scare me like that," Haruhiro snapped, looking at Kuzaku.

"Sorry."

The quick apology was fine, but Kuzaku was wearing a wry smile.

I can tell you aren't sorry at all, man, Haruhiro fumed. *I'm gonna have to knock some sense into you later. Not going to physically knock you around, though. Maybe a little lecture, I guess...*

"What were you getting so fired up over nothing for?" Setora demanded. "What are you, an idiot?"

Setora, who was less forgiving than Haruhiro, was clearly exasperated, and there was blatant disdain in her eyes.

Kuzaku seemed to finally realize the depth of his mistake, and began scratching his head and making excuses. "He was a really orc-y orc, so I couldn't help myself. Like, I have a hard time not seeing them as enemies."

"There are even more orcs here than in Roronea, you realize," Setora said coldly.

"Yeah, you're right... I know that, but... it just feels weird." Kuzaku had a look like he couldn't quite accept it.

Thinking back, they had gone into the Dusk Realm from the Wonder Hole, and then wandered into Darunggar and spent over two hundred days there. When they had finally managed to return to Grimgar, they'd arrived in Thousand Valley, a long, long way from Alterna.

Far too much had happened to them since then, and while they'd somehow made it to Vele, it had been a long trip. It was hard to imagine that it had been less than a year since they'd left Alterna.

Had they grown? There was no question that physically, and mentally, they had all changed. They had more experience, and had learned new things. Perhaps they had learned some things they didn't need to, or things they were better off not knowing.

It was true that orcs were the enemy. That was true now, just as it had been back then, but there was something Haruhiro knew now.

Orcs were the enemy of the human race, but before that, they were living beings, just like Haruhiro and the rest. If humans and orcs just shared a common language, they could talk together, and maybe even come to an understanding.

Even with the undead, who he had thought of as no more than intelligent zombies, there were men like Section Head Jimmy of K&K. Jimmy was someone they could absolutely get along with, and while they didn't have any orc acquaintances yet, they might find one they could be friends with someday.

Naturally, if they were enemies and it was necessary, he'd take the lives of orcs, or even humans, if he had to. Haruhiro had dirtied his hands before, so he wasn't about to talk about feeling guilty. If he had to, he'd kill without hesitation. It was kill or be killed.

But was it really necessary?

Were they really an enemy he absolutely had to fight?

The world wasn't big enough for both of them, and they had to kill one another. He had believed that all this time, but maybe... maybe that wasn't true.

Grimgar *of* Fantasy *and* Ash

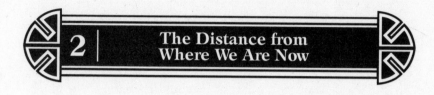

2 | The Distance from Where We Are Now

WHATEVER THE CASE, first they had to get back to Alterna.

However, the distance from Vele to Alterna as the crow flew was still five hundred kilometers, so they weren't close; they were actually rather far.

Naturally, considering the topography, they couldn't travel in a straight line, so it would be a journey of six to seven hundred kilometers. If they estimated six hundred for now, and then did their best to walk thirty kilometers a day, it would still be twenty days.

That was a fair distance. It was really far.

The area north of Vele was under the control of orcs and the undead, but Alterna was southwest, so they wouldn't be traveling through enemy territory. However, they had no knowledge of the local area, and didn't even know the general route back, so it might be hard to get back to Alterna on their own.

They had money. They had the one hundred platinum coins they had received as payment from the K&K Pirate Company. It was worth an incredible one thousand gold. It was so much money that, honestly, it didn't feel real.

Even though Haruhiro had a hard time believing it, they had the genuine article in their hands, so they considered hiring a guide, but he felt like they'd be taken advantage of. Well, they had a whole thousand gold, so it wouldn't matter how much they were overcharged, but it would be hard to tell who they could trust.

If people learned how incredibly rich the party was, it was possible that no end of people might plot to relieve them of that wealth, so it was best to pretend they were poor volunteer soldiers. They had to be at least that cautious.

Apparently merchants traveled between Vele and Alterna. If they looked around, there had to be a caravan or two looking for guards.

Or so he hoped.

"Am I maybe... being a little overly optimistic?" Haruhiro murmured.

He and the party gathered information from the proprietors and customers of stalls, as well as friendly passersby, and they finally ended up at Winged Ogrefish Street.

The entirety of the large, covered street was a marketplace, but there were hardly any shops with wares on display. It was primarily a place for the merchants to trade with each other, so it was lined with the offices of trade associations and companies.

It turned out there were multiple trade caravans going to Alterna. But when they asked the merchants leading them if they were in need of guards, none of them were friendly.

"Guards, you say?" One pudgy merchant with a marvelous mustache looked dubiously at the party with a nasal laugh. "Do you take me for an imbecile? If you ever do find a man who is fool enough to take on total unknowns such as yourselves, do tell. I am sure his idiocy would make a fine story to contemplate over a drink sometime."

That was harsh.

Kuzaku came close to snapping, but looking at it from the merchant's perspective, it was a reasonable stance to take. For the same reason that the party couldn't hire a guide so easily, the merchant wanted people he could trust as guards.

Looking more closely, there were many merchants traveling with well-armed men and women, and any proper caravan likely had mercenaries on retainer.

It didn't look like things would be as simple as expected, but, well, there was absolutely no need to rush.

They had money. Honestly, having money was wonderful. It gave them room to work with.

Haruhiro managed to secure some pretty nice lodgings for the party before sundown, and then they headed back out to get dinner together.

"Let's go to the Stormy Petrel Restaurant," he suggested.

In the process of gathering information, that place had come up a number of times as having good food.

When they arrived, they found that the Stormy Petrel was an outdoor eatery with over a hundred tables, but not a single chair. Customers were apparently supposed to buy food and drink at one of the numerous stalls nearby, then stand to eat and drink wherever they liked. There was a wide variety of dishes available, and they could get alcohol, too.

It was awfully busy considering the sun hadn't gone down yet, and the tables were nearly all taken.

Kuzaku and Setora were tasked with buying food, while Haruhiro, Shihoru, and Merry stayed at the table they chose. Kiichi went with them.

The gaps between tables were relatively small, and it was pretty noisy, so it was hard to relax when the place was so crowded.

"Should we have gone somewhere else?" Merry asked casually.

"Hmm." Haruhiro scratched his head. "I wonder. I mean, right now, we could go to the kind of luxurious restaurants we've never been in before. Like... I dunno. Something quieter? Maybe?"

Shihoru ducked her head a little and smiled wryly. "I feel like it might be hard to relax there, too..."

"Yeah. You might be right. We'd be out of place. Clearly."

"Not good enough for a dragon rider?" Merry asked with a teasing smile.

"Lay off with that, please..."

"It's how we got rich, though."

"It was pure coincidence. I didn't even ride the dragon, okay? I was just holding on for dear life. I mean... I'm shocked I didn't fall."

"That was—" Merry puffed up her cheeks almost like Yume for a moment. It was only a moment, though. They quickly deflated, but Haruhiro thanked the heavens he hadn't missed that moment.

What were the heavens? Like God, or something? He didn't really know. But it was a good face she'd made. Like a reward to him.

—Wait, how was it a reward?

"You get one demerit," Merry said harshly.

"...I'm sorry." Haruhiro bowed his head.

He'd had the feeling he'd been given a demerit once before. Did that mean he had two demerits now? A thought occurred to him. What would happen if he kept accruing demerits?

"Hey, pardon me!" There was suddenly an awfully loud voice, and someone slammed a mug down on their table.

It wasn't Kuzaku, or Setora, and it obviously wasn't Kiichi. It was a man with strangely stiff hair. He wore glasses, and carried a large backpack. He had the well-worn clothes of a traveler, and his boots were filthy, too. He looked human.

"...Huh?" Shihoru looked frightened. It seemed, at the very least, Shihoru didn't know who this guy was.

Well, of course not. If this were Alterna, maybe, but this was Vele.

Merry pulled Shihoru closer to protect her, glaring sharply at the man.

"Hm? Is something wrong?" The man's large eyes blinked behind his glasses. He had a snub nose, and his angular face was distinctive, in a way, but Haruhiro really didn't recognize him.

"Um... Who might you be?" Haruhiro asked hesitantly.

The man lifted his mug, chugged his foamy drink, and exhaled contentedly. "Me?"

"Well, you and us are the only ones here..."

"Wahahaha! We are, indeed! We are, indeed! I, you see, am a humble trader by the name of Kejiman. There were no seats to be found, and you people, you don't seem to be a large party, so I figured you wouldn't mind sharing the table. Look, it's just me by my lonesome. I won't get in the way. Right?"

"No, I'm not so sure about that..."

"You said it!" Kejiman laughed raucously again, then took another sip of his drink.

His laughter was mildly annoying. Also, it was sort of aggravating to see a little foam left around his mouth. It would have been fine to tell him to wipe it, but Haruhiro felt like that would be admitting defeat.

"We have more friends with us," Merry told him in an incredibly cold tone.

But Kejiman assured them with a seemingly endless supply of cheer, "It's fine!"

If he wasn't even flinching at Merry's rejection, he was tough. This guy, he had way too much mental fortitude. Was it that, or was he simply insensitive?

"You say you have friends, but it's not like it's ten or twenty people, right?" he asked. "In that case, I see no problem here. I mean, look at this table. Seven or eight people can use it, maybe even ten if you stretch it. How many friends do you have? One? Two? Three, maybe? Ohh, two! It's all good, then!"

Not good. Haruhiro was getting steamrolled here. If only Kuzaku or Setora were around. But those two weren't back yet. Haruhiro had to shut this guy down somehow.

—But wait.

"...A trader, you say?" he asked cautiously.

"Yes. Why do you ask?" Kejiman still had foam on his upper lip.

Damn, thought Haruhiro. *I lose.*

"Um... There's foam on your upper lip."

"Whooooooooops!" Kejiman wiped his mouth with the back of his hand, on which he wore a fingerless leather glove, his face turning red with embarrassment.

That embarrassed him? That was a long "whoops," too. Way too long.

"Sorry, sorry," Kejiman said. "And? Where were we? Oh, right, I'm a trader. What about it? From the looks of you, you're volunteer soldiers from Alterna. Am I wrong?"

"Well, you're not wrong."

"Yeah. Yeah. I knew I could trust my eyes. Or my glasses, at least. They're not just for show, you know. They're prescription. And? What? Were you interested in business?"

"Not particularly..."

"Oh, I see. It happens sometimes, you know. Former volunteer soldiers trying to go into business. The amateurs. I know a number of them. Well, it never works out, though. Serves them all right! Diiiiiie!"

"Isn't that a bit much...?"

"Sorry, sorry! I can't help it! The resentment builds up over time, you know!"

Slowly, Haruhiro asked, "Have you ever been to Alterna?"

"I have. I have. This is just between us, but I'm about to go again, too."

"Huh?"

"Oh, what do I have to hide? I'm making good money trading with Alterna!"

"The way you're shouting, I don't think you're hiding it at all..."

"Oh, that's just a thing I say sometimes. 'What do I have to hide?' It's a convenient expression. In other words, I'm the one who makes a quick buck on niche products no one else will touch! The great Kejiman, that's me! Wahahaha!"

3 | Way of Life

PERHAPS SHE WAS A WORRYWART. Always thinking things would get worse and worse. Especially when it came to herself, things would go badly. She couldn't help but think that way.

In truth, sometimes things went well, and sometimes they didn't. It went both ways. But the times it went badly were the ones she remembered. They stayed with her, never leaving.

If she reflected back upon the path she'd walked, not everything that had happened along the way made her want to avert her eyes. She understood that perfectly fine. But even when she raised her head, her face remained lowered in her heart.

For now, her actual face was facing down, too.

A droplet of water fell from her hair and landed in her lap.

"Shihoru."

Hearing her name, Shihoru finally raised her head.

The gentle light of a lamp illuminated the room. The inn itself was like a little castle, and upon first setting foot in this room, she had wondered what kind of princess must live here.

Of course, a princess's room wouldn't have had four beds in it. The furniture was minimal, too, and at close examination, the upholstery wasn't especially lavish. It was carefully built, regularly maintained, and kept clean, that was all. But the bed Shihoru was sitting on was soft, and there was a faint pleasant aroma.

How long had it been since she had stayed in such a place? This might very well be the first time.

Merry was standing in front of Shihoru, towels in hand.

"Your hair, it's still wet," she said.

"...Oh." Shihoru touched her hair. It was still rather damp.

Merry sat down next to her, pressing the towel against Shihoru's head. Her movements were careful, like Merry always tended to be.

You don't have to, Shihoru was about to say, but she swallowed the words. It was harder for her to accept kindness from others than it was to reject it. That was probably just her personality. Still, she had learned by interacting with friends that if someone wanted to do something for her, and that made them happy, she should let them, even if she wanted to hold back.

Yume didn't hide her feelings. She didn't lie. Shihoru was the opposite.

Even if she wanted to, Shihoru couldn't be like Yume. However, if Yume had snuggled up to her in search of warmth, Shihoru would hug her back and not run away. If Yume had said she liked her, Shihoru would somehow manage to respond, *Me, too.*

So even if she had trouble conveying how important the people she cared about were to her, Shihoru could still put her heart into her interactions with them.

"Thank you... Merry," she said slowly.

Merry smiled slightly and kept moving her hands.

Shihoru missed Yume's boisterousness. Now that she was alone with Merry, neither was particularly talkative, so they didn't engage in much small talk.

Shihoru didn't find silence unpleasant. She just worried whether it was okay to keep quiet, and what the person she was with would think. But while Merry spoke when she wanted to, she wasn't the type to force herself to engage in idle banter for no reason. So when Shihoru was with Merry, even if they weren't talking, it didn't feel awkward. They each told the other just what they wanted to, and listened to the words that came back.

"It feels lonely," Merry suddenly said.

"...Yeah." Shihoru nodded, and her chest tightened.

Merry felt the same way she did. She'd known that, though.

"It feels really... lonely," Shihoru said sadly.

"I feel like... Yume was always saving me," Merry sighed.

"Me, too. Maybe... no, definitely... even more than you, Merry."

"When she comes back, we'll have to welcome her with a smile."

"I might cry..."

"That's fine, though, isn't it?"

"I'm... a little angry." Shihoru hadn't meant to tell anyone, but the words just slipped out.

Merry let the towel rest on her lap, putting an arm around Shihoru's back.

Yume was pretty strong, but Merry was soft. For awhile now, Shihoru had assumed Merry was holding back. But she realized now she'd been wrong. This was Merry's way of doing things, and it was what made her unique.

"I was dumbstruck," Merry said. "It made me think, 'Yume's so funny.' I realized that all over again."

"She's too funny. But I'll admit, that's one part of her that, well... I love it."

The tears felt ready to flow, but they didn't. It was because Merry was staying with her.

"So, it never occurred to me she would go away..." Shihoru mourned. "I'm so creepy... I have this part of me. The way I'm so quick to depend on others."

"It's probably because Yume trusts you, Shihoru," Merry said comfortingly. "Even if she's away for a while, she's sure you'll be fine."

"Do you think Yume ever doubts her friends and comrades?" Shihoru ventured.

"I don't think so," Merry replied immediately, and she laughed.

Shihoru found that funny, too. "I know, right?"

"Even if she gets stronger, Yume will always be Yume. That's the feeling I have."

"She might change more than we think, you know..."

"Even if she does, that'd be so like her. I might just be fine with anything, in the end. As long as Yume is all right, and we can see her again in half a year, that's enough..."

Merry's right hand was on Shihoru's hip. Her left hand was playing with the towel above her knees.

"I guess... you're right."

Shihoru reached out with her right hand, grabbing Merry's left hand. She must not have expected it, because for a moment, Merry's body tensed. Still, even if she had tried to shake her off, Shihoru would have held on and not let go.

"Because you're here with me like this, I'm all right," Shihoru said. "No matter what happens, you're you."

Merry hung her head, thinking about something.

No matter how much they acknowledged one another, no matter how much they closed the distance, all people were separate. Shihoru hadn't been able to see through Yume's resolution. When it came to what was going on in Merry's head, she could only guess there, too.

Still, she could make the attempt. Even if she couldn't understand everything, she could at least tell Merry was deeply worried, and something was tormenting her.

Shihoru couldn't fix Merry's troubles. It might be difficult for her to even provide useful advice. Shihoru's very existence might not even be much help to Merry.

But—

I'm here, Shihoru thought. Even if you say you don't need me, I can't hate the friend I've trusted with my life, and no matter what happens, I won't give up. I'm clingy, and can be pretty creepy if I do say so myself, but there's no helping that. I mean, that's part of who I am.

"I'm glad," Merry said in a whisper, holding Shihoru's hand back.

What was she glad about? Shihoru chose not to ask, only imagining.

I should delve deeper, she thought. But she wouldn't do what she couldn't. She had her own pace, and couldn't become a person she wasn't.

When she'd first come to Grimgar, she hadn't even been able to measure her own steps. But little by little, stumbling forward, she'd at last begun to find herself. Lately, that was how Shihoru felt.

That was all the more reason why she was worried about Merry, who sometimes seemed to have lost herself. Holding her hand like this was all Shihoru could do. For anything more—

It can't be me, Shihoru thought. Haruhiro-kun. Probably... you're the only one who can do it. Do you understand that?

Suddenly the door opened, and Shihoru panicked. Merry sort of jolted away a bit, and Shihoru realized a moment later that she didn't really need to have panicked like that.

Setora came into the room.

Surprisingly, this inn had some impressively large gender-segregated baths. But it would be careless to leave the room empty, so Shihoru and Merry had gone to bathe first. Setora had stayed in the room while they did, then gone off to bathe alone, so now she was returning.

"Y-you... didn't take long," Shihoru said.

"Oh. Is that right?" Setora wiped her hair with a towel as she walked over to a different bed from the one Shihoru and Merry were sitting on. She took a seat herself.

They had all changed into cotton clothes bought in Vele's marketplace. They were simple garments that opened at the front, and unless they tied a belt around them, they easily fell open. They only went down to the knee, too, so they were a little exposed. Shihoru could never have gone for a walk like this.

Setora lay back on the bed, looking up at the ceiling. She took a breath. It might not actually have been the case, but Shihoru had the impression she knew what Setora was thinking.

She must feel uneasy right now.

When it came to Setora, there was always a wall between them. This place, the Golden Goatfish Inn, was a rather luxurious inn, and each room was five silver a night. That said, they had enough money to afford some luxury, and rather than getting just one room for the guys and one for the girls, they could have gotten individual rooms for everyone. Shihoru hadn't felt the need, but Setora surely felt constrained, so she should have done that.

"Let me just say this." Setora opened her mouth. "When it comes to the fact that I haven't managed to fit in with you people, you might think that I am not particularly concerned... but that is not the case."

Merry let out a slight, "...Eh?" and tilted her head to the side. It took Shihoru some time to register what Setora had said.

Setora lifted her legs. The hem of her garment slid, leaving her shapely legs completely revealed. What was she doing? She was slowly raising and lowering each of her legs. Was it an exercise?

"I am not good at getting along with others," Setora said. "Is that a poor way of expressing it? The practice of deepening my relationship with other people is one that I have hardly ever engaged in. Never, perhaps. Unlike golems and nyaas, the creatures known as people are difficult to handle. This may be a poor way of expressing it, too. Yes, I suspect so. I am not good at being considerate in the way I speak..."

Shihoru wondered if, for a start, she should tell her that when you're trying to word something delicately and be considerate, you don't tell the other person that's what you're doing. Still, it seemed Setora was doing her best to try and be considerate, in her own way, and that didn't feel bad.

"Um..." Shihoru said hesitantly. "Come to think of it, where is the nyaa?"

"Kiichi? He's exploring the city, I think. That one's a bundle of curiosity. It's unusual for a nyaa. Wild nyaas are not creatures that try to leave their own territory, after all."

"They're not suited to traveling?" Merry asked.

Setora stopped raising and lowering her legs. "...No. Not in their natural state. The nyaas kept by the village are used to moving, but they still mark the place they sleep with their own scent. It seems they can't relax otherwise."

Merry nodded, satisfied with the answer. She might have tried to think of another question, but she apparently couldn't come up with one. Shihoru had nothing, either.

Setora went to raise her legs again, but stopped midway. She was left staring up at the ceiling with her knees up.

The silence continued for a fairly long time. Of course, perhaps it only felt long to Shihoru, and it wasn't in fact that long at all.

"I selfishly brought them with me from the village, and let a large number of nyaas die." Setora covered her face with both hands, letting out a sigh. "I am a bad master. I broke Enba, too. I'm not sure I can fix him. I've no intention of returning to the village for now, so there's little hope of it."

Shihoru and Merry looked at one another.

What now? Shihoru wondered. What... do you think we should do?

Yume would have reassured Setora without hesitating. Whether or not the person was one of their comrades, whether or not they were even of the same race, none of that mattered to Yume. She could sympathize with others, and if she felt something, she was quick to admit it.

Shihoru, and also Merry, couldn't indiscriminately care for others the way Yume did.

"With humans..." Was Setora crying? Her voice wasn't trembling. It was fixed and emotionless, as usual. "...they have a public face, and a private one. They hide their true feelings behind a facade. They lie. Easily. Even to themselves. I thought it was unsettling as a child, but not so much now. Everyone has things they want to protect, and they're all desperate. It's just that I can't deal with all of that. I'm not interested enough... or so I thought. I had

Enba, I was surrounded by nyaas, and that was enough. It should have been enough. Did I make a mistake? Well, I have no regrets."

Setora paused for a moment.

"I hadn't realized it, but once I left the village, I was glad to be free of it. The village was constraining, but I had never thought of leaving. Now, I find that strange. I wonder why. Why did I never try to leave the village? Was I afraid? Uncertain? ...Regardless, I have now left the village. I have no desire to return. Unless I go back, I cannot rebuild Enba. Still, I do not want to return. I feel bad for Enba, but not bad for me. How should I say this? I feel alive. I've never felt so alive."

"Is it fun?" Merry asked, and Setora removed her hands from her face.

"...Fun. It might be, or it might not. Despite having lost Enba and the nyaas, I'm not all that disheartened. There is not much I am dissatisfied about."

"But... there are some things?" Shihoru asked hesitantly.

Setora was monologuing at them, and Merry and Shihoru were just asking questions to confirm what she was saying. It felt like an awkward form of communication, but this was likely the best they could do at the moment.

"...Yes," Setora said. "I might call it a dissatisfaction. To be blunt, there are times when I feel something like a sense of exclusion. I think, most likely, I am indeed feeling excluded. Having been shunned by the house I was born into, I am used to it, so it's not that much of an issue. From the time I was born, I was defiant, not submitting to the house as I should have. I knew what would happen as a result, but I did not want to be my parents' slave, and I would not give in to the ways of the village. Now... I am not so stubborn as I was back then. Though, that said, I am not seeking a compromise from you. To give an example, I find Haru pleasing, but I will not ask that he find me pleasing in return. That would be the wrong approach. Even if I were to force him to obey me somehow, his heart would not turn towards me. Just as I never obeyed my own house. That is because, priest... Merry... Haru, he loves you."

To think she'd actually come out and say that now! Shihoru looked at Merry out of the corner of her eye.

Merry had gone stiff. A statue. She had turned into a statue.

It was hard to imagine she hadn't known, but, in a way, Merry might be even more dense than Yume about those sorts of things, so Shihoru wanted to feel her out to be sure.

I just want to be like, "Hey, your feelings are reciprocated, you know." If I did that, how would Merry respond? She might say, "Why?" with a look of surprise on her face.

They were always together, so she forgot sometimes, but Merry was so beautiful that people found her difficult to approach. She was shapely, too, and honestly, Shihoru was jealous of that, but being so different from the norm must have come with its own troubles.

It seemed Merry had little experience with romance, was disinterested, and was also rather dense. Haruhiro-kun, too. Not only was he not super experienced, he was kind of juvenile, maybe?

Did that mean they were both still children emotionally, then?

Shihoru had begun to suspect, if they were left to their own devices, that maybe things would never go anywhere.

Should I do something? How would I even go about trying?

Shihoru wasn't exactly experienced herself. Actually, all she had to work with was a one-sided crush and her fantasies, so she wasn't likely to be much help.

Setora sighed, then mumbled to herself, "...Things just don't work out."

"I know, right?" Shihoru agreed, looking over at Merry, who was still completely frozen up.

Honestly, all sorts of things aren't working out. It feels like I'm walking an endless tightrope, and sometimes jumping down from it would be easier. But I probably never will.

Shihoru had too many things she wouldn't want to let go of that easily. No matter how she treasured them, she could lose them at any moment. Now might be the only time that she could keep holding on to them.

Yume has her own way of living, so I think she had to go away, Shihoru reflected. But I want to see you, Yume. Even though we only just parted, I want to see you so badly.

"So, to sum things up, each of us is burdened with our own personal issues," Setora said, smiling just a little.

Without a word, Shihoru mentally added:

Yeah—and we're alive.

Grimgar
of
Fantasy and Ash

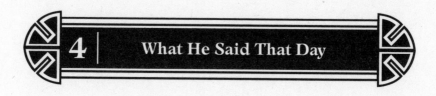

4 | What He Said That Day

"I MEAN, there's something weird about him, right?" Kuzaku asked. "That Kejiman guy. I'm sure of it."

Even once they turned the lights out and the room was completely dark, Kuzaku and Haruhiro kept talking about stuff that didn't matter. Or rather, Kuzaku was doing basically all the talking, and Haruhiro was just nodding along. He was pretty tired, after all.

"Well, yeah," Haruhiro said.

"But, well, then again, if he weren't a little weird, I'd think something was up."

"You've got a point."

"He doesn't seem like he's totally on the ball. More like he's a bit out of it."

"Yeah," Haruhiro said.

"But hey, he could just be faking it. Like, we could be getting a fast one pulled on us here."

"Gotta be careful, huh?"

"I'll let you handle that part, Haruhiro. As for me, well, you know."

"Yeah."

"Zzz..."

"Kuzaku?"

"Zzzzzzzzzzz..."

"Man, you sure do fall asleep quickly..."

Not like I care, really. Haruhiro turned over in bed.

The window was still open. There was a slight breeze. It was still a bit hot, though, so he just had a thin blanket over him up to his belly.

It hadn't really hit him when he was on the ship, but now that they were staying in an inn like this, he felt rich, and that made him uneasy.

A thousand gold. It was hidden under the bed right now. What should he do about it? If they carried it around with them, he worried it would be stolen, or perhaps strange people would gather around them.

That wasn't very good from a mental health perspective, so he wanted to just blow it all on something, but that wasn't something Haruhiro should just decide on his own. Besides, was there even a proper way to spend it?

For example, even if they ordered Kuzaku a full set of custom-made armor, it wouldn't even cost a hundred gold. With a thousand gold, they could buy a house and have money to spare. They could probably even buy a ship.

That said, houses and ships were of no use to volunteer soldiers. They couldn't manage such things themselves, and it was stupid to just keep paying the upkeep on them.

"...We could quit. It's not like it isn't an option," he dared to whisper to himself.

Kuzaku was breathing softly in his sleep.

They had a full thousand gold, after all. Even if they set Yume's share aside and divided it six ways, that was a hundred and sixty-six gold apiece. He didn't know if that was enough to fool around for the rest of their lives, but if they weren't stupid with the money, they could live comfortably for ten to twenty years on it.

Ten to twenty years might be too long, but taking it easy for a year or two wouldn't be bad. Why had no one suggested it?

They had promised to meet Yume half a year from now in Alterna. That said, there wasn't anything saying they had to stay active as volunteer soldiers during that time.

They'd go to Alterna. Meet Yume in half a year. Other than that, they were free. They could enjoy an extended break.

If they were going to retire from being volunteer soldiers, that was a big deal, so it might be a good idea to move away and do something else for a while. However, none of them, Haruhiro included, seemed to be considering that.

Yes, Haruhiro wasn't, either. He was just running through all of the possibilities in his head to be sure. They would likely keep working hard at the volunteer soldier trade, just like they had been all this time.

But how long could they keep it up?

If he recalled correctly, Akira-san of the Day Breakers was in his forties. He'd been a volunteer soldier for upwards of twenty years. Two decades.

How many years had it been since the woman called Hiyomu had led Haruhiro and the others to the Volunteer Soldier Corps Office? Five? Six? No, no. It felt like it had been eons ago, but it had actually been fewer than two years. The thought of doing this for twenty years was mind-boggling.

Another eighteen years of this, huh?

Honestly, he couldn't see them surviving it. What was the survival rate for volunteer soldiers? It couldn't be that high. Haruhiro had been in enough situations where he could easily have died.

Enough? No. More than enough.

Having stood at the brink of life and death too many times, he'd developed an ability to avoid danger. He hoped that was true, but Haruhiro just had a brush with death again recently.

Naturally, he wasn't taking risks for the thrill of it, and he was being as cautious as he could, but it still kept on happening.

Occasionally, he'd think about it. Eventually, in the not too distant future, he was likely going to die.

He might not die. He might notice one day that, like Akira-san, he had been a soldier for twenty years, but it was overwhelmingly more likely that something like that wouldn't happen.

It wasn't like he wanted to die young. So if he was going to live a long life, he had to call it quits at the right time.

Akira-san wasn't a genius. That was what his comrade Gogh had said about him. He was no genius. Akira-san had just survived.

Having been lucky enough to survive, Akira-san had been given time. And so, he'd gotten strong.

He hadn't survived because he'd gotten strong. He'd gotten strong because he'd survived.

"But they can say whatever they want," Haruhiro murmured. "I mean, it's all stuff they're making up after the fact."

Even assuming Haruhiro did survive, could he get strong like Akira-san? Haruhiro had taken things seriously, hanging in there at the brink of death all this time, so he knew. People were not equal. There really were such things as inborn potential, talent, and limits to one's abilities. Looking at the whole picture, Akira-san was clearly extraordinary, while Haruhiro was ordinary.

Perhaps even a mediocre person like him could, with a surplus of luck, survive twenty years as a volunteer soldier. Well, he couldn't rule the possibility out, at least. But as for becoming a legendary volunteer soldier like Akira-san, it would never happen. No way, no how.

But, to Haruhiro, that wasn't what was important.

Haruhiro didn't want to get rich or famous. He wouldn't disagree if someone said he could stand to be more greedy or have more ambition, but he wasn't going to overstretch himself for those things. If they never came his way, that was fine.

The issue was, even if Haruhiro did survive, his comrades might die. Tomorrow, Kuzaku, who had just started snoring in the bed next to his, might breathe his last and become a cold, dead body.

Haruhiro got up. The bed creaked a little. Kuzaku stayed sound asleep.

Haruhiro put on his shoes, got out of bed, and quietly left the room.

Lights were out in the hall. It seemed there were still lamps lit off by the stairs, and the light was shining this way.

The place they were staying, the Golden Goatfish Inn, was a four-story building. The second through fourth floors were all guest rooms. The rooms on the second floor were quad rooms, this third floor was for double rooms, and the fourth floor had large guest rooms with multiple smaller rooms inside.

Unlike in Alterna, there were plenty of four and five-story buildings in Vele.

Haruhiro descended the stairs to the second floor. Without meaning to, he glanced at the door to the room where the girls were staying. Were they all asleep by now? Or were they awake and talking?

Shihoru and Merry were fine together, but how had adding Setora changed the mood in there? Shihoru and Merry were both quiet types, so it was hard to imagine there was a roaring conversation.

"If only Yume were around..." he murmured.

Haruhiro passed by the girls' room without a sound, opening the door at the T-junction at the end of the hall. There was a wooden deck beyond it. He'd had a premonition somewhere in his head that someone might be there, but there was nobody.

"What am I getting my hopes up for?" He laughed to himself

a little as he gripped the railing. Then he let out a sigh.

The Golden Goatfish Inn was in a quiet, stylish area, and he could see the lanterns of the guards on patrol from the deck. The tight security was one of the selling points of the many inns and hotels in this area. It wasn't just the objects in them; security also had to be bought with money, or else secured by one's own means.

Haruhiro rested his elbows on the railing and his face in his hands. In such a big city, there had to be a good number of professional thieves. There could be armed robberies and murders, too. Someone could be being murdered right now, and it would be utterly unsurprising if, at this very moment, a person or two was about to die of illness.

And besides that, even if you defended yourself properly, and tried to take care of your health well enough, there was no fighting back against a natural disaster that no one saw coming.

Even if they weren't volunteer soldiers, they'd die when their time came. That was true, but in this trade, they could make enough money to make up for the amount their lives would be shortened.

No volunteer soldier wanted to die, but they knew that they had to take on risks while stopping short of actually dying.

Eventually, Haruhiro would grow numb to it. No, he already was pretty numb.

Thinking about it, when first starting as a trainee volunteer soldier, he'd been far more timid than he was now. Even an unarmed mud goblin had been unbearably frightening to him.

"Lives are at stake here!" Manato had shouted.

Those words... Haruhiro had completely forgotten them. Lives were at stake on both sides in the volunteer soldiering business. It was full of challenges that couldn't have more serious stakes.

"There's no way it's going to be easy... huh..." he murmured.

No person, no living being, wants to die, Manato had said. Then, although he couldn't have wanted to, Manato had gone and died ahead of the rest of his comrades. That was where it had all started for Haruhiro and the others.

How far forward had they come from that place that now felt so far away?

"No, that's not it..." he murmured.

They hadn't actually progressed at all.

They had just one life, and if they died, it was all over. That principle would not change for anything.

There was no changing it, so even if they improved their skills, or were taking on more challenging opponents, in essence it was all the same. They were creatures that didn't want to die killing other creatures that didn't want to die, feeding on them, profiting, and going through the joys and sorrows of life.

If that felt sinful, he'd long since given up and accepted it.

He wasn't into stepping on those he killed and basking in the afterglow of the deed, but he didn't think it made him a better person to not do so.

He stole a creatures' only life from them, without being tortured by any sense of guilt or responsibility, and even if it should have left a bad aftertaste, he didn't even feel it anymore.

Well, it's the same for us. We put our lives at stake, and just happen to win. If we lose, we die. The conditions are the same, so we'll be on the other side eventually.

He might have thought something selfish like, *We each only have one life, so no holding any grudges.*

"But..." Haruhiro pressed his head to the railing.

But what if that wasn't true?

Grimgar of Fantasy and Ash

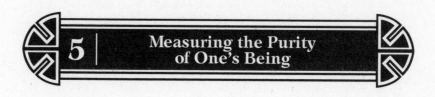

5 | Measuring the Purity of One's Being

SOMETIMES, I just don't know. Sometimes? All the time? It may not be a matter of frequency. How often? Is it important?

It's nothing to think about so deeply. You'll get used to it. You can get used to anything.

Shut up. Shut up. Stop.

What? Stop what? I'm not doing anything.

Yes, you are. You are.

You're imagining it. I'm not doing anything. No one is. I won't get in your way. Because I understand. I've been through this, too. Okay. You should try calming down. Take a deep breath. Nice and easy.

I can't control my pulse. It beats whether or not I do anything. I can't stop it by my own will.

My breath. I can control my breath. Breathe in. Breathe out. Breathe in. Breathe out.

Stop.

Stop. Stop. Stop. Hold it like that. Stop. Keep holding it. Does it hurt? Well, it's fine. You're okay. You won't die. No, that's an imprecise way of saying it. That's not enough for you to die. Your life is like a heart. There's nothing you can do about it yourself. Soon enough, you'll come to accept. You'll gradually begin to understand. What all this is. Right? Right. You can get used to anything. So long as you're living.

Living.

It's best not to contemplate whether this counts. That's something everyone's thought, after all. It's stupid to repeat the same thing over and over. A waste of time. Some feel it's okay to waste a little time. Well, sure. I suppose it might be.

Stop.

I'm not doing anything. Nothing, really.

Stop.

It's nothing to worry about.

Stop.

It's like a heart, after all. You have time.

Stop.

Stop.

Plenty of time. Time to adapt. You can accept this. Because you have no choice but to. There are easier ways, too. It might be all right to choose a simpler path. I'll teach you. If you want to know.

What?

...What is it?

I can't say I recommend it.

Yeah. I don't recommend it.

But it will make it easier. Breathe in.

Breathe out.

Breathe in.

Breathe out.

Breathe in. Breathe in. Breathe in. Breathe in.

Breathe in. Breathe in. Breathe in. Breathe in.

Breathe in. Breathe in. Breathe in. Breathe in.

Breathe in. Breathe in. Breathe in. Breathe in.

Breathe in. Breathe in. Breathe in. Breathe in.

Breathe in. Breathe in. Breathe in. Breathe in.

Does it hurt? Then you can stop.

Give it up.

You don't need to control it.

You can throw it away.

—What?

What can I throw away?

You know, don't you?

It's your self.

My self?

It's fine.

Nothing bad will come of it.

Well, of course not. You won't even be able to feel things are bad anymore.

It'll be easy. It'll set you free.

You suffer because you think you are there. Affirming that you are there every moment, it's pretty exhausting, isn't it?

Because you have to keep affirming it.

Like stabbing yourself with a needle.

Prick, prick, prick.

It's a thin needle, so holding it is a lot of effort.

It's possible you may drop and lose sight of it.

Your self. Your self. Your self. Your self.

Your self. Your self. Your self. Your self.

Your self. Your self. Your self. Your self.

Your self. Your self. Your self. Your self.

Your self. Your self. Your self. Your self.

Your self. Your self. Your self. Your self.

Your self. Your self. Your self. Your self.

Your self. Your self. Your self. Your self.

Your self. Your self. Your self. Your self.

Your self. Your self. Your self. Your self.

Your self. Your self. Your self. Your self.

Your self. Your self. Your self. Your self.

Your self. Your self. Your self. Your self.

Your self. Your self. Your self. Your self.

Your self. Your self. Your self. Your self.

Your self. Your self. Your self. Your self.

Your self. Your self. Your self. Your self.

Your self. Your self. Your self. Your self.

Your self. Your self. Your self. Your self.

Your self. Your self. Your self. Your self.

With each moment, that needle stabs into the back of your hand somewhere. There's no need to work so hard. It's a lot of effort, right?

If you get tired, you can rest.

Don't push yourself, rest.

Rest.

Rest now.

Rest.

Come now, rest.

Stop.

I open my eyes. Even if it's dark, I can see. Take a breath. Breathe.

In.

Out.

In.

Out.

In.

Out.

Even if I can't control my heart, I can control my breathing. I can sense it. That I am here. The one controlling my breath, that is my self.

My self. My self. My self. My self.

My self. My self. My self. My self.

My self. My self. My self. My self.

My self. My self. My self. My self.

My self. My self. My self. My self.

My self. My self. My self. My self.

My self. My self. My self. My self.

My self. My self. My self. My self.

My self. My self. My self. My self.

My self. My self. My self. My self.

My self. My self. My self. My self.

My self. My self. My self. My self.

My self. My self. My self. My self.

My self. My self. My self. My self.

My self. My self. My self. My self.

My self. My self. My self. My self.

My self. My self. My self. My self.

With each moment, I affirm my existence, like stabbing in a needle.

I exist.

Here.

I am here.

Someone look at me. Hear my voice.

Feel me.

Hold me.

Please.

Sometimes, I just don't know. Sometimes? All the time? It's not a matter of frequency? How often? Is it important? It's nothing to think about so deeply, I think. Because I'll get used to it. I can get used to anything. At this rate, I will end up getting used to it.

So look at me. Hear my voice. Feel me. Hold me. Please.

But I don't want to use you like that.

I am impure.

6 | If You're Going to Travel

HER NAME WAS ZAPP.

There was one very prominent horn on her sturdy head. Her face was big and oval-shaped. Her thin eyes looked nothing if not peaceful, but who knew if she actually was.

Her movements were relaxed, and she was mild. She was hairy, but her tough, brown hair wasn't all that long.

Her body was huge. Taller than Kuzaku. What was more, Zapp wasn't even standing up.

A ganaro was a quadrupedal creature, so it wasn't common for them to stand on their hind legs, but this one was still big.

Ganaroes were raised widely throughout Grimgar as livestock. Humans, orcs, and other races had tamed ganaroes since long ago, using them for milk, meat, or labor. They were a common animal, so Zapp felt familiar.

She was an especially large ganaro. At first they thought she was male, but she was actually female.

Kejiman stroked her strong neck and smiled as he introduced her. "This is my partner. She's like a wife to me. Hahahaha!"

Did he mean that as a joke? It wasn't clear, but Haruhiro wasn't going to laugh.

The boxy four-wheeled cart Zapp pulled was rather small, but it had spring suspension. It was called the *Vestargis-go*.

It had a crew of one. It looked like you could cram three people into the coachman's seat, but Kejiman said it really only sat one.

In addition to Zapp, Kejiman brought a bird named Nipp with him. Nipp was a kind of large, flightless bird called a storuch.

There were wild storuches living in the Quickwind Plains, but they were not used to orcs or humans. Only this domesticated breed, produced through the tenacious use of selective breeding, would let humans and orcs ride it.

Still, it was important to never stand behind a storuch. Because they would send you flying with an incredibly powerful kick.

"Nipp is my friend, I guess," Kejiman grinned. "The only friend I need. Hahahaha!"

He deliberately stood behind Nipp, showing off this neat trick of his where he dodged a powerful kick by a hair's breadth.

"Even I have a hard time getting out of the way. If you don't retreat immediately, there'll be a second one coming, too. If you take two in a row, it'll nearly kill you. I speak from experience here. Wahahaha!"

With that said and out of the way, it was now the party's job to protect the merchant caravan consisting of Kejiman, Zapp the ganaro, Nipp the storuch, and the four-wheeled cart *Vestargis-go* on their twenty-five day journey to Alerna.

Food and water were provided, and he would pay them thirty silver each. Kiichi the gray nyaa would, by the way, not be counted towards that.

Kejiman's initial offer had been a daily allowance of one silver, making it twenty-five silver per person. It was hardly good pay, and it would have seemed unnatural to accept it easily, so Haruhiro had made a point of at least haggling.

"Now, listen, my life is on the line with this trade," Kejiman warned them. "It always is, though."

After holding out as long as he could, Kejiman offered thirty silver, saying he could go no higher, on account of not having the money.

"I put almost everything I have into stocking up, you see. There's no way I'd have money to pay you people. If I hadn't met you all, I was thinking I'd be fine going alone. I'd've had no choice but to go it alone. What will you do? Will you go? Will you not go? I'm fine either way. It's up to you people. Do as you please!"

As per their first impression, this guy was nuts. He was a bit nervous to do it, but Haruhiro didn't want to be taken advantage of, so he kept on haggling, and they finally agreed that once the cargo was sold in Alerna, there would be a bonus.

The Gate of the Sea God in Vele opened at half past six o'clock in the morning. They set out not long afterwards, taking an unmapped route to the southwest.

Kejiman sat in the coachman's seat of the *Vestargis-go,* and Nipp followed behind despite not being tethered to it.

Haruhiro and the party were on foot. While making very sure that they didn't end up behind Nipp and get kicked, they kept on walking.

The humble merchant Kejiman's trade caravan ignored the perfectly fine road paved with whitish stones, the White Road, and instead crossed fields, forests, and hills to push southwest.

That it was better than Darunggar went without saying, but it was also better than Thousand Valley or the Kuaron Mountains. Even if they did nothing but walk for twenty-five days, that was an easy trip by the party's standards.

"Man, there's nothing out here..." Kuzaku mumbled to himself, and Kejiman laughed nasally.

"We'd be in trouble if there was. I'm going out of my way to avoid places people go. Now listen, I'm about to say something obvious, but it's because you people are ignorant. I'd like you to hear me out with that in mind, but there are a million thieves and bandits in these parts. I say a million, but I don't mean a literal million. That would be way too many. Still, there are a lot of them. I've been hit a number of times myself."

It seemed Shihoru, Merry, and Setora, who had Kiichi with her, were ignoring whatever Kejiman said unless it was important. They didn't even respond.

Haruhiro know how they felt. The guy was kind of... infuriating, yeah. Haruhiro would have preferred not to listen himself, but the guy was their employer, so he couldn't ignore him outright.

"So that's why you've developed your own route," Haruhiro responded.

"That's right. Light, the Raiders, the Crush Underdogs, Dashbal... there are all these famous groups of thieves and bandits. If they find you, and think you've got something of value, it's over."

"Light..." Haruhiro murmured.

"Light is a group of volunteer soldier drop-outs. If you ask me, humans who've ruined themselves are far more villainous than either orcs or the undead."

"...Oh, yeah? Is that how it is?"

"Orcs, they're pure, I guess you could say," Kejiman said. "There's something refreshing about the way they act. It's a bit harder to figure out what the undead are thinking, but they don't act cruel for no good reason. The ones you really need to watch out for are humans who've gone astray."

"Right..."

"Still, though, even with scary guys like Light, it's not like they'll just show up out of nowhere to kill, rape, and pillage."

"...Yeah."

"Ha! 'Yeah,' he says! What's your problem?! Come on! Get involved in the conversation! I'm making an effort to talk with you here!"

I'm not getting involved in the conversation because I'm not that interested in what you have to say. Haruhiro wanted to say that, but couldn't. It might be satisfying to, but it was sure to cause trouble.

"...Do they threaten you?" Haruhiro asked at last.

"They do. Well, hey. I guess you're interested, after all."

"Do I look that way?"

"There! That's the way to be!"

"...Huzzah."

"Threats are their usual modus operandi. 'You pay us this much, we won't attack,' they'll say. I'm sure that larger caravans with a proper defense force can just tell them, 'Bring it on!' though. That's why the thieves and bandits don't attack those sorts of caravans. Everyone values their own lives, after all. In the end, it's the medium and small ones that get hit. For an independent trader like me, I have to get by on my wits and courage alone. I'm looking for a wife, by the way!"

"...I see."

"I mean really looking for a wife! I'm super, super looking for one! How about it?! There's a seat open beside me, you know?!" Kejiman slid over, patting the spot beside him.

The women in the group were freezingly silent.

"Hahahaha! It's fine, it's fine. Pure, innocent men like me who are pursuing their ideals – women hardly ever understand us. It's fine. Just fine. When it comes down to it, I can just buy them!"

"That's pretty scummy," Kuzaku let slip.

Kejiman erupted in an instant, standing in the coachman's seat. "Hey, you! Who're you calling scum, you handsome bastard?! Don't get all full of yourself just because you're tall and good-looking!"

"Nah... I'm not that full of myself."

"Yes, you are! You so are! Let me tell you, me, I've never once been popular with the ladies! The number of people I've gone out with, zero! Still, if I just pay, even a man like me can have his needs satisfied! This is reality! Even if they don't love me, I have people who'll pretend they do! If I pay, that is!"

"...Erm. Listen, I'm sorry."

"You pity me?! Even my own father never pitied me!"

This was going to be the first of a long twenty-five days. Haruhiro didn't even want to think about it.

But, well, it wasn't like he had no tolerance for men like Kejiman. Besides, once they reached Alterna, it'd be goodbye. If he considered this a limited-time thing, it would be easier to put up with.

On the first day they walked twenty-five, twenty-six kilometers over the course of half a day, making camp at the base of a small mountain.

Even when he slept, Kejiman stayed in the coachman's position. Haruhiro and the rest pitched tents, taking shifts on watch. They heard the cries of nocturnal beasts, and sensed their presence, but the morning came without further event.

Kejiman being annoying aside, the second day also went well. The third, too. When things were so uneventful, that was actually worrying.

That night, Haruhiro slept lightly even when not on watch. In the morning, he had a short dream. Yume showed up out of nowhere, and she wanted Haruhiro to be a target for some reason.

Well, if you insist, he said, and acted as a target for her.

Yume took aim and fired arrow after arrow at him, but they all narrowly missed.

They're not hittin', huh? Yume laughed.

They're really not. Haruhiro laughed, too.

But I've got a feelin' the next one'll hit, Yume nocked an arrow and drew back the bowstring.

Just as Haruhiro thought, *Oh, this one's going to hit the bullseye,* he woke up.

What a dream...

On the fourth day, they had a good time cutting across the fields, climbing gentle hills, and ambling through quiet forests. It really was peaceful.

They reached the climax of the first stage of the journey a little after noon that day. They got to the edge of the forest, and there was a river.

Kejiman jumped down from the coachman's seat and ran forward. "Yahooooooo! We're here! The Irotoooooo...!"

"This is..." Haruhiro rubbed his cheeks and chin. He had a bit of a beard going. It was pretty thin, though. He'd have to shave it.

"It's big..." Shihoru murmured.

Maybe the sparkling surface of the water was too bright, because Shihoru was squinting. No, it was cloudy today, so it wasn't sparkling at all. She must have been confused.

"I wonder how wide the river is..." Kuzaku cocked his head to the side.

Yume would have been able to eyeball it with a reasonable amount of accuracy, but Haruhiro could only tell vaguely.

"Two hundred... Three hundred... More, maybe," he said at last. "It could be four or five hundred meters."

Obviously, if they were traveling along the ground, there were going to be rivers. They had crossed a number on the way here, but none had been further than waist-deep for Haruhiro, and their currents hadn't been fast.

Kejiman had warned them in advance they would be crossing a river today, but he hadn't mentioned that this Iroto was such a major river.

Nipp went into the shallows, drinking the river water eagerly. Tied to the *Vestargis-go* a short distance from the riverbank, Zapp looked a little jealous.

Kejiman was playing around, skipping flat rocks across the surface of the water.

"What is with that man?" Setora muttered. "Is he an idiot? I suppose he is."

Setora skillfully removed the yoke keeping Zapp fixed to the *Vestargis-go*. Now Zapp could move about freely.

Zapp gave Setora a short cry of, "Bumo!" before slowly walking toward the bank. She stuck her face in the water, and drank. She was gulping it down.

Beside her, Kiichi wet his hands and rubbed his face.

Seeing that made Merry smile. Well, when a nyaa washed its face like that, it was cute, after all. Yeah. It was the sort of thing that'd make you smile.

But moving on.

Shihoru made a gesture with her chin. "That guy..." she said, indicating Kejiman. "I don't believe he said the river wasn't crossable. How do you think we're crossing it?"

"Thirty-five skips!" Kejiman threw his hands up in delight. It seemed the stone he'd thrown had skipped thirty-five times across the surface of the river.

"Dammit," Kuzaku said, clicking his tongue. "Seeing that, it makes me want to try, too."

"You can," Haruhiro said. "If you really want to."

"Stop it, Haruhiro! If you tell me that, I'll seriously end up doing it."

"Do it, man."

"But if I do, you'll look down on me. You'll think I'm the same as that guy."

"No, I won't."

"I'll do it, I'm serious! This is no good. I'll hold back. If you ended up looking down on me for something like this, man, I wouldn't be able to go on living."

"You really don't need to worry about how I see you..."

"Well, I do!"

"Thirty-seven skips...!" Kejiman called.

Kejiman had kept throwing small stones, and it seemed he had a new record.

What's he fooling around for? Haruhiro wondered. *It looks super fun. I... don't want to do it. I'd never do it.*

"Umm..." he began, trying to get the man's attention.

"Hold on!" Kejiman shouted as he pulled back his arm, then threw yet another stone. The stone skipped across the surface of the lake, almost as if it were sliding, and then sunk into the water. "Yessssssssssssssssss!" Kejiman shouted and pumped his arm. Thirty nine skips! I win! Zeeeeeeeeeed...!"

"Zed...?" Haruhiro repeated. He knew it was better not to say anything, but he did.

Kejiman turned back, using the middle finger of his right hand to push up his glasses. "Me! I won! In a competition against myself!"

"No, not that. What's zed...?"

"Heheheheh..." Kejiman suddenly burst out laughing. "Wahahahahahahahahahaha!"

He laughed loudly. Like an idiot. There was something wrong with him. Haruhiro had thought he was weird from the beginning, but the man kept on being even more of a weirdo than anticipated.

He'd have to consider his options. Like abandoning Kejiman and running for it, maybe. *Was it too early for that?* he wondered.

Looking over to Zapp, Setora and Kiichi were riding on her back.

"Um... Er..." Haruhiro began.

"Hm? What is it?"

"No, don't ask me..."

"Oy, oy, oy, oy, oy?! Zapp is *not* a vehicle!" Kejiman shouted, looking off to the side. His face was a mask of anger, but Setora seemed unaffected.

"She's an animal, after all. I see no reason to think she would be a vehicle."

"Then why are you riding her?! What for?!"

"I thought I could, so I did," Setora said. "Is that wrong?"

"I should ask, how do you think it's not, zeeeed! By the way, I feel like I can say it easily now, so I'm gonna announce it, but we can't cross the river here! We should've been able to, though! We should have! But it looks like not! How regrettable!"

Shihoru's jaw dropped, and she blinked repeatedly.

Merry's face tensed for a moment, then she smiled for some reason afterward. It was a little scary.

"What's that mean?" Kuzaku asked, then a few moments later, his eyes went wide. "Huh?! Wh... What do you mean? Whuh...?!"

"You're way too shocked..." Haruhiro sighed.

It was a surprise, though, sure. He was starting to get a headache.

"This is why you were goofing around," Haruhiro said. "I knew something seemed off..."

"Well, sorry." Kejiman bowed his head with a beaming smile.

If he was going to apologize, he could try to look more apologetic. Why did this man do things that rubbed people the wrong way? It was hard to understand.

"So, what do we do?" Setora made no attempt to get down from Zapp. Well, in this situation, even if Kejiman was going to snap and demand she get down, Haruhiro didn't think she had to.

Kejiman picked up a small stone, throwing it at the river. It was an upwards toss, so the stone fell into the water without skipping.

"Yeah, that there. That's the problem..."

7 | Stop Time

THEY ONLY HAD KEJIMAN'S WORD to go on for this, but there was apparently a tribe known as the Kyuchapigyurya who had lived in the Iroto River basin since long ago, and Kejiman was coincidentally acquainted with a group of them.

Kichipigira. No. Was it Kyuchapigyurya? The name was hard to pronounce, and it sounded made up, but they made a living hunting and fishing. Fishing, in particular. They got on boats, using traps, nets, and harpoons to catch fish, crocodiles, and turtles.

This was all according to Kejiman, so he was sure it was a bunch of baloney, but the great Iroto River was home to vicious turtles that could be over two meters long and man-eating crocodiles, so even just fishing there meant putting your life at risk.

These Kyachupiginya—no, Kyuchipiryagya—no, wrong again, Kyuchapigyurya—lived in this area, and Kejiman claimed to have crossed the Iroto on their ships twice. He said they would carry Nipp, Zapp, and the *Vestargis-go* on their boats.

They were apparently fond of alcohol, but could only make simple moonshine themselves. So when he offered them distilled liquor, they were quite pleased, and they'd help him as if it were no big deal.

"That's why, look, I went to the trouble of bringing alcohol! What do you think?!" Kejiman pulled a bottle of liquor out of the *Vestargis-go*, holding it up high for them to see.

He seemed so desperate that it only came off as more fishy, but it mattered little now whether Kejiman was lying.

These Kyu-whatevers he said had lived here before weren't here now. There was no visible sign of them having lived here. Naturally, it would be impossible to enlist their aid in crossing the river.

And they couldn't very well try to swim across a river infested with two-meter turtles and man-eating crocodiles. The *Vestargis-go* would probably just sink, anyway.

For now, sitting around here would do no good. When Haruhiro and the party started having a constructive discussion about whether to move on, Kejiman stopped sulking and throwing stones into the river, perked up, and came over to poke his head in.

"Upstream or downstream? Do you want to decide which way to go? Should we play rock, paper, scissors? Compete to knock over the opposing team's pole? Do a stone-throwing contest? I'll take you on at anything! Bring it!"

It would be rude to tell their employer he could shut right the hell up, so Haruhiro asked him more tactfully, "Could you please keep your mouth closed for just a little bit? I don't want to make this any more complicated."

"What, it's my fault?! You're saying this is my fault?!"

"Yes," Setora shot back. "This is entirely your fault."

Setora was still on Zapp's back, and Kiichi was resting between her horns. It seemed Kiichi liked it there. Zapp wasn't protesting, either.

Kejiman had tears in his eyes. "I have *never* felt so *humiliated!* More! Be harsher! I welcome the abuse! No, please abuse me! Please!"

"What is this vile piece of trash, and why does he continue to make an embarrassment of himself by continuing to draw breath?" Setora muttered.

"Wha?! I want to take that one down in the notebook of my heart! Memoryyyy!"

"Let's go upstream," Haruhiro suggested. "If we go downstream, we're bound to hit the sea eventually."

No one objected to Haruhiro's proposal.

Kejiman was a total weirdo, and it was stressful not having the trip go as planned. That said, they weren't facing any pressing crisis at the moment, so everyone was calm. That was reassuring.

It was decided Setora and Kiichi would sit in the coachman's seat of the *Vestargis-go*, and Kejiman would walk. He was, technically, their employer, so Haruhiro questioned for a moment if it was okay, but Kejiman was now in Setora's utter thrall.

Zapp had taken to Setora, too, making the pace of the *Vestargis-go* steady, so it looked like it was fine. Still, Setora could do just about anything, huh...

Setora's caravan headed upstream along the Iroto. No, it was

Kejiman's caravan, really. But seeing Kejiman walk cheerfully beside Zapp as she pulled the *Vestargis-go*, he was clearly her underling, her servant, or her slave.

If Setora were to tell him, "You are now my slave now. Submit," Kejiman would instantly reply, with a flash of his glasses, "With pleasure!"

Is that okay? I dunno... Yeah. I guess it is.

Eventually, the riverbank took on the appearance of a dense forest. The trees tried to impede the *Vestargis-go*'s advance, but it was fine.

"This way!" Kejiman called. "This way, Setora-san!"

Each time the *Vestargis-go* came to a stop, Kejiman found a route around and beckoned to them.

Each time Kejiman did something good, Setora never failed to, in an emotionless tone of voice, say, "Well done," giving him that small bit of praise.

"Yes, Setora-san! I'd do anything for you, Setora-san!" Kejiman cried.

If Kejiman had a tail, it would be wagging constantly. He was totally her pet.

Was this the technique of a nyaa master at her finest? Setora was terrifying. To think that she could even tame humans. Either that, or this was just something Kejiman was into, a fetish. That might well be it.

On the fourth day, they made camp atop a small hill. For caution's sake, Haruhiro and Kiichi looked around before it got dark out, but there didn't seem to be any danger.

The party had handled all the cooking up until this point, but Kejiman now insisted he do it, so they opted to let him.

"Me, I want to let Setora-san eat my cooking," Kejiman said. "No, I wish her to do me the honor of eating it. Do you understand, Setora-san? Will you do me the favor of understanding?"

"No, I do not understand at all."

"You're so cold, Setora-san! But still, that's what I like! Are you the best?! You're the best! Weeheeeeee!"

Incidentally, Kejiman's cooking was surprisingly advanced, and it wasn't totally disgusting. Actually, it tasted good.

"How is it, Setora-san?!" Kejiman asked, a sparkle in his eye.

"Not bad," Setora replied curtly.

Kejiman rolled around in glee. He was thrilled. Never had Haruhiro seen a man so happy.

Honestly, it was creepy, but depending on how you looked at it, being able to express joy so wildly might be enviable.

No, Haruhiro wasn't jealous of him, after all.

Under their contract, the night watch was to be performed by the five members of the party, and Kejiman was exempted. But now Kejiman very much regretted this, and he insisted on a change in contract.

It was blatantly obvious he wanted to be on watch duty together with Setora. Naturally, Setora was having none of that.

Kejiman looked as if every hope he had in life had been crushed, and immediately went to cry himself to sleep.

"Whew, today was something else," Kuzaku yawned. "I'm exhausted..."

"Yeah," Setora said curtly. "That was awfully exhausting."

"I know, right?" Shihoru agreed. "It really was exhausting..."

Kuzaku, Setora, and Shihoru all requested their watch come after they had slept a little. As a result, Haruhiro and Merry ended up taking the first watch.

It was clear they were trying to be considerate. But if possible, he'd have preferred they stop this weird way of doing it. Still, maybe, in fact, it only came across to Haruhiro as them being considerate, and he was just misunderstanding. If so, that was pretty embarrassing.

For now, he'd have to pretend everything was normal and do his duty of keeping watch. Merry didn't seem any different from usual, after all.

The two sat across the fire, facing one another. That was to prevent blind spots. This way, their field of vision covered 360 degrees.

If he was being honest, Haruhiro wanted to avoid facing Merry straight-on like this. When he was right in front of Merry, she was guaranteed to be in his field of vision. He couldn't help but look at her.

It was hard for him to look at Merry's face, now illuminated by the fire, directly. Once he looked, he couldn't tear his eyes away. He was entranced.

It was weird, staring at a comrade's face for a long time. In fact, it was abnormal. He shouldn't look so much. But he couldn't help it. It troubledoubled him.

What? Troubledoubled? Was it double trouble? Was that it? No. Not at all.

Anyway, the point was that it troubled him.

He couldn't afford to be troubled. If Haruhiro was troubled, Merry would feel even more troubled. He didn't want to trouble Merry.

They were no different from usual, with aimless conversations that went nowhere and then suddenly trailed off, only for one of them to speak up again. As usual, they went back and forth, ran out of things to say, and fell silent.

It was awkward when the silence went on for too long. He was working to prevent that. Still, even the times when neither was talking weren't bad in and of themselves.

Was that just an excuse, and was he only trying to justify himself? Well, at this point, he didn't care.

"They say wellness starts in the mind, after all..."

He didn't know what had led up to that line, and even thinking back, he really didn't have any clue.

"That's true..." Merry's gaze hung in the air, as if she were staring off into the distance.

Had he just said the wrong thing? But why was it a bad thing to say? He had no idea.

Merry smiled just a little.

"But everyone is helping," she said.

"Oh, yeah? ...Yeah. We're comrades, after all."

Merry nodded wordlessly.

We're comrades, after all. Haruhiro pondered that. *We are comrades, right? We are. We're comrades. Not just comrades, though, I think. I think that's true with my other comrades, too, though. We're not just comrades. We're something more than that, you could say.*

I mean, I think it's weird that I'm still thinking things like this. If Kuzaku and the rest weren't being needlessly considerate of us, I wouldn't end up having to think like this. There are times when the best of intentions can backfire, and lead to the opposite result, okay? I know. I'm taking this out on the wrong people. But still, nothing's going to happen here, okay? I mean, there's no way to make it happen, all right?

"I think I may take a look around over there," Haruhiro said, getting up.

"Alone?"

"...Huh? Uh, yeah... alone. We can't leave this place empty, after all..."

Even as he said it, he questioned the need to go look around. Yeah, it was unnecessary. So why had he said that?

Being alone with Merry...

Is it painful? No, it isn't, okay? I don't know what to do, and my chest feels tight because of it. It's not pain, though. I feel restless. That's all.

"Well, I'll be here," Merry answered. "Take care."

For a moment he thought, *Is she mad?*

Looking at Merry, she was smiling. He didn't seem to have hurt her feelings. Thank goodness.

Haruhiro stood up. He tried to walk off.

His feet wouldn't move.

What was the matter?

He scratched his head. He sat back down again.

Then he stood back up.

"Is something wrong?" Merry asked.

"Yeah..." Haruhiro sat down. "I don't think I'll go, after all..."

"Okay."

"...Yeah." He let out a sigh.

Do I need to change something? he thought. That, or do I have to change? If so, how should I change? What should I change?

"What do you figure Yume's up to now?" he ventured.

"Sleeping, I'd guess."

"Oh, yeah... I suppose she would be, huh."

"Are you worried?"

"Well, yeah, I guess I am worried. I'm sure she'll be fine, though. I mean, it's Yume."

"Yeah. If anything, it's us..." Merry started to say, then trailed off.

"It's us..." what?

It bothered him. Should he ask? Why couldn't he ask?

Haruhiro sniffled. He looked at the fire. There was some hint hidden there, and he was confident that if he squinted, he would discover it. That was a lie. He wasn't confident at all. There was no way he'd find a hint. In the end, the fire was just a fire.

"Man, I'm always just waiting..." Haruhiro mumbled in an incredibly small voice.

It wasn't like he was hoping Merry would hear it. Could he say that for certain? He might actually have been hoping. He was so gutless.

"Haru. Did you say something, just now?"

"Oh... no..." he said hastily.

It's pretty terrible of me to act like I never said anything, isn't it? he reflected. *I just have to not pretend, that's all, but I can't stop trembling in fear.*

"I think... I'm not assertive enough..." His voice was, in fact, trembling.

"Because you're a nice guy, Haru."

"Do you really think that?" he asked, despite himself.

Merry was facing downwards. He'd asked her a question that was difficult to answer.

Haruhiro rubbed his left eyebrow. The inside of his mouth felt awfully dry.

Wow. It was amazing how parched he felt.

"I'm... not able to see myself as nice, or whatever..." he said finally. "It's different. I'm not nice... I think. I dunno. I'm just trying to avoid problems, I guess? I feel like that's where it comes from..."

"Nobody wants to make waves, you know? If things are good, and you don't want them to change, you'll want them to stay as they are."

I see, Haruhiro thought. *To sum it up, Merry is satisfied with the status quo, and wants to maintain our current relationship. Is that it?*

Yeah, that's gotta be it. That's the only way to take it. If I were to interpret her meaning, she's saying, "Don't come any closer." In a "know your place" sort of way. There may have been times our bodies touched, but those were coincidences, so I shouldn't read too deeply into it. "Let's forget all that," is that it? That's what it means, right? Basically?

Yeah.

I thought so.

Whew.

Maybe this was for the best, actually? I caught myself before there were any weird misunderstandings. That sure was dangerous. Close call. I could have really badly embarrassed myself there. If I messed up, I could have made a fatal mistake there. I might have messed up badly. In fact, I can guarantee I would've.

Haruhiro stood up. His body felt strangely light. Or rather, his legs were weak, and everything seemed vague and blurry.

"I'm gonna go look around."

"...Huh? You're going, after all?"

Haruhiro gave her a vague smile. Why was he smiling? Even he didn't know.

Hang in there, me. If I just start walking, it'll be like a switch was flipped, and everything will become clear, like I've switched into a new mode, I'm pretty good like that, he thought. *I can still keep going. I'm pretty young, after all. I've got a lot ahead of me. I'm sure I probably do...*

Now, it's time to stop thinking about things that don't matter. I have things in front of me that need doing. Focus on them. But what are they? Looking around? Is that it? Is that something that I really need to do? Not really, right? But I will. That's what living is all about. Most likely. Probably. I guess...

Haruhiro walked. His footsteps made no sound. No part of

his body made any noise. Even his breathing was suppressed to the level it was imperceptible.

He melted into the darkness. Became one with it. It felt good. Really good. His Stealth was working. He felt like he'd become a Master of the Night.

What was a Master of the Night? There was no one like that, huh? They didn't exist.

There's something. A sound.

There was almost no wind tonight. The insects were chirping. The birds were occasionally making noise, too. As for the babbling of the river, they were camped pretty far from the Iroto, so he shouldn't have been able to hear it.

Just what is this sound?

Haruhiro had long since descended the hill on which they'd made their camp. Even so, he was only two, three hundred meters away. The Iroto wasn't this way; it was likely in the opposite direction.

Why had his feet led him this way? It was half unconscious, but he understood the reason why.

The sound. Haruhiro was drawn in by this mysterious sound.

It was so very difficult to describe. It was hard to compare it to anything. However, somewhere, at some time, he had heard a very similar sound to this.

Is it a musical instrument, maybe?

What kind of instrument could it be? An instrument?

In a place like this?

This could be kind of dangerous... couldn't it?

Haruhiro felt like he had as good a sense for danger as anyone. Was it time to turn back?

If he were traveling alone, he'd have done so without hesitation. But though he hadn't planned for this, he was a guard for a caravan, and he was on patrol right now.

Was it really dangerous? How so, and to what degree? He had to find out, and respond with a full grasp of the situation. He was the leader, even if he wasn't much of one. Haruhiro had a responsibility.

With that sound as his guide, he swam through the darkness.

For a time, quite a while, actually, he hadn't been able to get into Stealth, like he was in some sort of slump. But heartbreak...

Is it heartbreak? he wondered. *Going through the shock from an experience that is similar to, incredibly close to heartbreak, may have gotten me over it. I'm making the best of a bad situation. Good and bad luck are closely interwoven. Where there's bad, there's good, and where there's good, there's bad. Things can't always be good, but they won't always be bad, either. Thinking of it that way, it gives me courage. Yeah. I think I can go on like this. Damn straight I can. I can do it. I am doing it.*

It's a little bright up ahead.

Is it opening up, with the moonlight shining down? The sound I hear is coming from there.

There's no need to be extra cautious. I'm already cautious enough.

Haruhiro moved forward.

It's not what I thought. It's not opening up. There's a depression. It's getting lower.

At the edge of the depression, Haruhiro came to a stop. He was a little unnerved.

There's a tent.

It was a big, round tent. He'd never seen one so big. There were multiple entrances, each covered by a curtain, but a little light was leaking out from inside.

There was a little spring in the depression. Those animals with their heads thrust into it, were they horses? They were horse-sized. But maybe they were different animals. There were several of them. He could see animals further away from the spring feeding on the grass, too.

The source of the sound was that tent. Was it from some musical instrument? Someone was playing music.

This is bad, isn't it? he wondered. *No, maybe not?*

I wonder.

Grimgar of Fantasy and Ash

NATURALLY, Haruhiro headed back, shook everyone awake, and informed them of what he'd seen.

Kejiman seemed to ooze cheer from his entire body, and was ridiculously excited. "Y-y-y-y-y-y-y-y-y-y-y-you! Do you know what that is?! You don't, do you?! You can only act so calm because you don't! Unbelievable! Do you lack basic, common sense?! Or are you an idiot?! I'll bet you're an idiot, a big damn idiot!"

"...I'm pretty sure I haven't done anything to merit that response."

"The massive tent that appears by night! Mysterious music! This is a famous story, you know! Everyone know it, unless they're an idiot or live under a rock! Which are you?!"

"I don't know..."

"You can't even answer that! That means you're an idiot! Well, not that it matters! Whether you're an idiot or live under a rock, it doesn't make a difference! That's a minor detail, so let's get going!"

As Kejiman tried to take off running, Setora grabbed him by the collar.

"Hold up."

"L-Let go!" Kejiman squealed. "You're choking me! It hurts! I'll suffocate! I'll suffocate to death!"

"If you'd like, why don't you go ahead and suffocate?"

"Noooooooooo, thank you! I still have things I need to do! No, I can't die until I see the Leslie Camp for myself! I could never rest in peace otherwise!"

"Leslie Camp?" Kuzaku cocked his head to the side. "What's that?"

"U-u-u-u-unbelievable! You really don't know?! You're pulling my leg! I can't believe this! You can't *not* know about the Leslie Camp! You must literally live under a rock!"

He was saying that, but this was the first Shihoru or Setora had ever heard of it, and it was the same for Haruhiro.

What about Merry? He couldn't ask. While it hadn't been outright suspicious, the way Merry reacted had been a little odd.

"Have you... heard of it...?" Shihoru asked her in Haruhiro's place.

Merry hesitated for a moment before nodding. "Just the name," she answered briefly.

"Ohh," Kuzaku said with a relaxed nod. "Merry-san, you might disagree with us sometimes, because you've had a longer career than the rest of us."

Oh, yeah.

That was right.

Merry was kind of their superior—no, not just kind of; she had definitely been a volunteer soldier longer than the rest of them.

The Leslie Camp. From what Kejiman said, it was a fairly major thing. It wasn't weird that Merry would know. Haruhiro and the rest were just ignorant.

That had to be it. No doubt about it.

"I don't mind going to see, but it's not dangerous, right?" Haruhiro asked carefully.

"Is it dangerous?!" Kejiman exclaimed. "Does worrying about that let you live a more fulfilling life?! Can you sing out loud about how wonderful this life is like that?! Don't you think there are more important things out there?!"

Kejiman babbled on, explaining the Leslie Camp had been sighted in places all over Grimgar, usually by night. It was apparently a regular feature of accounts that claimed that it suddenly appeared where there had been nothing during the day.

As one might infer from the name, a person called Leslie was involved with it.

Ainrand Leslie. He was the master of the Leslie Camp.

Some said he was human; others said he was undead. He was a merchant who had been famous in certain quarters for over fifty years.

That said, he was more than some mere merchant. Ainrand Leslie acquired objects the likes of which no one had ever seen, and would sometimes hand them over in exchange for a great price. Sometimes in gold, sometimes in other forms.

One rich man in Vele turned his beautiful wife and daughter over to Ainrand Leslie without regret, and received a ring unlike any other in this world with the power to call storms.

However, then the rich man had no idea how to call storms. So when he asked Ainrand Leslie for help, this was the response:

"Let me teach you. However, the price will be your new wife."

The rich man had a young mistress. He had resented his wife who was past her prime, and his daughter, who was cheeky with him. For the rich man, his original wife and daughter had been no great price to pay. In fact, he'd been able to rid himself of them, gain the ring, and marry his new wife. Three birds with one stone.

But his new wife...

"As if I would give you my wife!" the rich man snapped and threw the ring down on the ground.

When he did, a storm arose, dark clouds forming as people watched, and Vele was hit by a great storm of heretofore unseen proportions.

Houses collapsed, and many ships sank. Ainrand Leslie vanished, and the rich man perished inside his ruined mansion.

There were countless such tales of Ainrand Leslie. That said, he wasn't a person from hundreds of years ago, so it was much too soon for there to be legends of him.

According to Kejiman, there was no shortage of people who claimed to have met Ainrand Leslie. There were quite a few people in Vele who would show off some oddity, treasure, tale, or piece of junk, or try to sell it, claiming they had received it from Ainrand Leslie.

However, there was not actually any solid proof, nor any unshakable evidence that Ainrand Leslie had definitely visited Vele. The story of the rich man was seen as a delusion, a fabrication, something idiots would talk about over drinks.

Even so, no one questioned that Ainrand Leslie existed.

Here was another story, for example.

A young girl ran away from home, wandering into a forest not ten kilometers from Vele. The girl was eventually drawn to a mysterious sound, and came across a large, round tent, with horse-like creatures gathered around it. She turned back in fear, wandering the forest until morning, and somehow made it home.

The girl told everyone around her about the things she had seen. Someone suggested it could be the Leslie Camp, and with rumors giving birth to more rumors, there was soon an uproar throughout Vele.

For a period of over ten days, hundreds of people—no, thousands, or perhaps tens of thousands—headed out into the forest, seeking the Leslie Camp.

In the end, the camp was not discovered, but this had happened just five years ago, so most people in Vele remembered it.

Travelers who wandered Grimgar, curious adventurers, exvolunteer soldiers, merchants burning with ambition who would go anywhere for profit, none of them encountered the Leslie Camp. If it could be found by searching, someone would have by now. There were those called Lesliemaniacs who obsessively traded information on it among themselves, but it was said that the more you looked, the further away the Leslie Camp got.

Regardless, the Leslie Camp was obviously the place to find Ainrand Leslie. He was one of Grimgar's few collectors.

He might not have had a ring that called storms, but he might have one or two famous treasures like a red diamond, said to be worth enough to buy an entire country, or a solid gold bust of Enad George, the founding king of Arabakia, or the lost crown of the royal house of Nananka, or the Necklace of Nigelink, which Princess Titiha of lost Ishmar had worn until the moment of her death, or the Dawn Scepter, or the treasured sword Ulgis.

If anyone were to attempt to buy any of those famous treasures, Ainrand Leslie would no doubt demand an extortionate sum. However, even if they could not have those things, even a glimpse of them would be a story they could tell until the day they died.

Also, hardly anyone took this seriously, but there were childish stories that Ainrand Leslie could grant a wish for anyone who met him.

Furthermore, according to one theory, Ainrand Leslie was neither human nor undead, but something akin to a fairy or spirit, and could bring great wealth to people with his mysterious powers.

In truth, the reason no one who claimed to know his face came forward was connected to that. Those who became rich with the help of Ainrand Leslie would carry that secret to their graves. Just like money, if everyone had good fortune, it would decrease in value. That was why, until they died, they were better off hiding what they knew about Ainrand Leslie. That was the secret to ending a privileged life still at the top.

Did the Leslie Camp ultimately exist? If they were to judge purely based off what Kejiman said, it was a little dubious.

No, really dubious.

However, Haruhiro had seen it with his own eyes.

That being the case...

Honestly, though he wasn't enthusiastic about the idea, he guided his comrades and Kejiman there.

They soon arrived.

Haruhiro hoped that, after following the route he remembered, they'd be disappointed to find it was no longer there. It wasn't that he wanted to be disappointed, but if the Leslie Camp existed, he didn't see it being anything but trouble. He wanted to avoid that... but it didn't work out.

This might be a major find, but he wasn't happy about it in the least.

"Th-th-th-th-th-th-this is...!" Kejiman stood at the edge of the depression, pulling on his own hair. He was pulling so hard that his glasses fell off. "Ohhh! M-my glasses! Where, where, where are my glasses?! My glasses...!"

"...Here." Shihoru picked them up and returned them.

Kejiman put them on and rushed towards the bottom of the depression. "Ohhhhhhhhhh! I! Am! Leslie! Camp!"

"You're the Leslie Camp now?" Kuzaku asked. "Wait—"

He glanced over at Haruhiro as if to say, *Don't we need to go after him?*

It was questionable. Maybe they didn't? Haruhiro was apparently not the only one thinking that, because Shihoru, Merry,

Setora, and Kiichi the gray nyaa didn't move from the edge of the depression, either.

Haruhiro and the party were only hired as guards. They weren't Kejiman's mommy or daddy. They didn't have to go along with this.

"If that man were of no further use, now would be the time to cut him loose," Setora said quietly.

She could say that again. She had a point. Setting aside the bit about him being their employer, they needed him to lead them back to Alterna.

"Heyyyy..." Hesitant to yell too loudly, Haruhiro called after him with a half-hearted shout.

Either Kejiman didn't hear, or he wasn't listening to begin with, because he didn't stop. He didn't even turn back. Seriously, what was with that guy?

He was already reaching the bottom of the depression.

Guess there's no other choice, huh? Even if I ran my fastest, I couldn't catch him in time.

Haruhiro steeled himself. They would stand by, and wait to see what happened. If it got ugly, they'd have to leave Kejiman and run.

Farewell, Kejiman. Until we meet again.

"Ahh..." Kuzaku groaned, then covered his mouth. He must have been worried about Kejiman who was at least making an attempt to creep as he approached one of the doors to the tent.

You're such a damn softie, thought Haruhiro. *But I do think that is one of your strong points. It makes you a likable guy. Still, it's that part of you that worries me the most. I know that may be none of my concern, though.*

Kejiman was already at a point around ten meters from the entrance to the tent.

"This sound," Shihoru whispered. "Is it an accordion?"

"That's it!" Haruhiro realized.

The image of a musical instrument composed of a snake-like bellows and a keyboard that could be pressed came to mind. Then he lost track of what he was thinking, and just the word a-kor-dee-on was left behind like an empty box.

This, again? He was getting mad now.

Now isn't the time to get mad, though, I guess...

Kejiman finally reached the door to the tent. He was sure Kejiman would be cautious from that point, but Kejiman suddenly flung the curtain open.

Should we run for real? For several seconds, Haruhiro seriously considered it.

"Ainrand..." someone said in a small voice.

No, not just someone.

Haruhiro reflexively looked to Merry, who was next to him. Merry's eyes were open wide, like something had surprised her.

Haruhiro didn't hesitate, and in the most subtle way he could manage, he averted his eyes. He didn't know if he could pull off acting like he hadn't seen anything, but he was going to try.

Kejiman poked his head into the tent. Was nothing going to happen?

Eventually, he started waving his hand. *Come on!* was what he apparently was trying to say.

Kuzaku looked around to the rest of them. "...Do we go?"

Grimgar of Fantasy and Ash

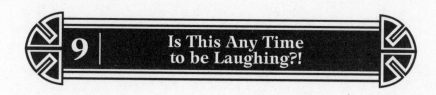

9 | Is This Any Time to be Laughing?!

PEEKING HESITANTLY into the tent, the only one there was Kejiman.

That was right. Kejiman had apparently been too impatient for Haruhiro and the rest to arrive, so he'd gone in ahead of them.

It wasn't wide. Three meters in each direction, maybe. It was divided not by walls, but lustrous, deep purple curtains. There was a red carpet laid out on the floor. Its fibers were pretty long. There was a side table standing in the corner, and atop it was a rather expensive-looking lamp. Considering the size of the tent, there had to be another room or something if they pulled back those curtains.

There was nothing like a musical instrument that could have been making the sounds they'd heard here.

Haruhiro had his comrades wait outside, setting foot inside the tent himself.

Kuzaku held the entrance open from the outside.

"This is truly... truly it," Kejiman said. Then he started to laugh. "Heh heh heh heh!"

"Listen, um... could you be quiet?" Haruhiro asked.

"What for?!"

"Do I really have to explain?"

"We're dealing with *the* Ainrand Leslie, you know! If he wanted to do something to us, he could have done anything, anything, anything by now!"

"You don't know what kind of person he is either, do you, Kejiman-san? Not even if he's human or not..."

"Buuuuut! I am confident that when it comes to rumors, gossip, hearsay, and more about Ainrand Leslie, my knowledge is second to none! Maybe second to none is a little excessive, but I'm decently knowledgeable about the subject! I know some things!"

"Isn't the level of knowledge you have gradually decreasing there...?"

"This roooom!" Kejiman stood bowlegged, pointing up diagonally with the index fingers of both his hands.

"Is there some meaning to that pose?" Haruhiro sighed. Haruhiro lamented his need to point these things out.

"This room iiiis...!" Kejiman cried.

Haruhiro was being ignored. Depressing.

"...the Violet Roooom!" Kejiman exclaimed, finishing his sentence. "From what I've heard, the inside of the Leslie Camp is viiiioleeeet! In other words! In other worururds! This labyrinth of deep purple curtains! The labyrinth really exists!"

"I'm already exhausted..." Haruhiro muttered.

"Okay, okay, let's calm down now."

Kejiman thumped himself on the chest twice, breathed out, and then cleared his throat.

Oh, man. This is bad news.

Haruhiro felt he was used to guys like this. That was why he had a way to control them to some degree. Or so he'd thought, but he had been pulled totally off his pace. There was always someone better than you. Who knew he'd been up against such a tough opponent?

"Now, come in, people." Kejiman gestured with his arm.

Kuzaku followed them inside the Violet Room.

Haruhiro pressed his hand against his forehead. "What're you coming in here for, man?"

"Ah! Sorry, I didn't mean to..."

"They have no choice but to come in, anyway." Kejiman pressed on the bridge of his glasses with his middle finger, letting out a low laugh.

"Why is that?" Setora flipped back the curtain to ask.

Kejiman lowered his voice and said, as if unveiling some special secret, "The thing is... there is a legend about Leslie Camp, saying, 'You cannot leave through the door you enter.'"

"Nonsense."

Setora passed through the curtain, boldly entering the Violet Room. The curtain at the entrance closed behind her. Then Setora made an about-face, attempting to leave the way she'd come in.

"Wha...?"

Setora was heading for the exit. There was no doubt about that.

If she reached out, she could reach the curtain. If she moved a little forward and pushed the curtain aside, she should have been able to leave. And yet...

"How strange," Setora murmured.

"What is it?" Kuzaku asked.

Setora shook her head as if she couldn't understand it. "I don't know."

"Ho-hoh! Well, well!" Kejiman attempted to run to the exit, but on the way he froze in place, and his entire body started twitching. "Nnnnngh...! Wh-wh-wh-wh-what is thiiiiiiis...?!"

"Huh? You can't get out? You're pulling our leg." Kuzaku laughed and headed for the exit. The first and second step went fine, but he came to a dead stop right in front of the exit. "What is this? All I can say is, it feels weird..."

Kejiman was one thing, but it was hard to imagine Kuzaku or Setora were messing with him. Haruhiro didn't need to try it himself; he could assume something abnormal was going on.

Shihoru, Merry, and Kiichi were still outside.

There were two options. He could have the Shihoru and the others outside escape, and those inside would figure a way out themselves, or...

No. Haruhiro shook his head. Splitting up the party was no good.

"Shihoru!" he called. "Merry and Kiichi, too... come in."

Two people and one nyaa came through the curtain into the tent. Merry seemed pensive, or had a slightly grim look on her face, but she looked like she might be pale, too.

Perhaps Kiichi sensed something, because he jumped up and had Setora hold him. Shihoru seemed uneasy, too.

"What's... going on?" Shihoru asked.

"Well, you see—" Kuzaku started to explain, but he was cut off by someone's voice.

"Helloooo. How are you feeeeling? Weeeelcome to the Leslie Camp."

"Nihah?!" Kejiman let out a weird cry and looked left and right.

"Just now... did that voice say Leslie Camp?" Shihoru asked.

Yes, Haruhiro had clearly heard the voice say that, too. Was this really, really the Leslie Camp? What did that mean for them? Whatever it meant, that voice...

That voice was a woman's voice.

He might have been imagining it, but it sounded familiar, or maybe not...?

"You are humans, yes? That means you understand this language, yes? Are you all—"

"There!" Kejiman turned to the left curtain, pulling it violently. When the curtain was pulled back, there was a similar room surrounded in curtains, and no sign of any person inside. "...Urgh! The voice was coming from here, so whyyyy?!"

"Oh, my, my, my, my," the voice said. "We have some lively guests here. Too lively, in fact. If you get too carried away, you won't live long, I'm afraid."

"Wh-where are you?! Come out! No, please come out! You, the one with the voice of a beautiful young girl!"

"Kyapii," the voice said. "How'd you know I was a beautiful

young girl, I wonder? From just my voice? Do I give off such a high level of beautiful young girl-ness that it can't possibly be hidden? But I can't."

"Why kyapii?!"

"O travelers." The self-proclaimed voice of a beautiful young girl suddenly took on a more august tone. "Seek and wander. If you do, your path will lead you somewhere. I welcome you once more, travelers, to the wandering warehouse of relics that my master, Ainrand Leslie has gathered."

The voice cut out.

Haruhiro and Kuzaku quickly traded glances. Haruhiro took the front, Kuzaku the right. They both pulled back the curtains in unison.

The room in front of them was no different from this one. But the room to the right was different. It had a wooden door.

Taking a glance at it, Haruhiro couldn't help but find it bizarre. Normally, doors were built into walls. However, that door stood with a curtain behind it.

From the look of it, if they opened the door, there would be a curtain behind it.

"Ohhhhh!" Suddenly, Kejiman rushed over in front of the door, and reached for the knob. If Haruhiro had reacted a moment slower, Kejiman would no doubt have opened it.

Spider.

No, he wasn't going to go as far as killing him. Haruhiro just pinned Kejiman's arms behind him before he could do it.

"H-hold on!" Haruhiro exclaimed as he struggled.

"Argh, let go! I'm your employer! What do you think you're doing to your employer?!"

"We don't know what will happen!"

"Whether it's a demon lord or a dark god that's going to come out, we won't know until we try!"

"Somehow, I don't really want either of those coming out!"

"Let go! Let go, let go, let go! No, no, no, no, no, no, no, no!"

"What are you, a petulant child...?"

Haruhiro handed Kejiman, who was flailing around and making a scene, over to Kuzaku. He felt safer for now, but what to do next?

"We can't go out that exit," Haruhiro pondered aloud. "If we can find another way out..."

"There is still no guarantee we will be able to leave." Setora was thoroughly stroking Kiichi's throat. Perhaps she was trying to calm him. "That woman's voice, it said this was a warehouse of relics. It was a relic that made creating artificial souls and manufacturing golems possible, too. Though this may not be true for all of them, a certain percentage of relics hold the power to upend the laws of this world. They are priceless."

"Theyyyy're! Iiiin! Heeeere! Lots of them! Even that door, as ordinary as it looks, muuuust be a relic!" Kejiman screamed.

Kejiman was being held firmly by Kuzaku. He wasn't gagged, though, so he could still shout.

Setora gave Kejiman a side-eyed glare. "What a noisy man. Should I silence him?"

"Y-y-you're going to kill me?! If so, I'll shut up for a bit..."

"Close your mouth until I say otherwise. You are insufferable."

Kejiman nodded in silence.

"That's a relic..." Shihoru was hugging her staff, looking nervously at the door, but not approaching it.

Merry was quiet. She looked down, her brow furrowed. Was she okay?

No, it wasn't just Merry; none of them were okay.

"Could we just open it, open it and see what happens...?" Kuzaku asked.

His suggestion was worth considering. They could try opening it, and if anything weird happened, they could immediately close it again.

"No," Haruhiro said. "But, hmm, I'm not sure..."

Like Kejiman had said before, they had no idea what might come out, so honestly, he was scared. Still, Haruhiro deliberately swallowed his fear, and decided not to use the word "scared" anymore, if possible.

It was good to have a sense of fear. It made him cautious. But wailing about how scared he was could only hurt him.

Even if it was baseless, he had to, at the very least, reassure his comrades that they could handle this somehow.

"For now, why don't we check out the rest? Obviously, we'll do it as cautiously as we can, though," Haruhiro suggested with feigned calm.

No one objected.

10 | ROOMS

EACH TIME HARUHIRO pulled back a curtain, he tensed both mentally and physically.

That was for the best. It was at the times when he was sure that they were fine, and nothing bad would happen, that things tended to go wrong.

"A box, huh..." he murmured.

In this room, in addition to a side table and lamp, there was a box large enough he would have to wrap his arms around it to pick it up. It didn't seem to be made of wood. It was probably metal.

Kejiman tried to touch it, but Setora shouted, "Hey!" at him.

"Eek! I'm sorry!"

This was becoming a regular occurrence.

It was unclear if this box, or the door from earlier, were relics, but for as long as that remained a possibility, it was best not to touch them carelessly. Having encountered the mysterious phenomenon that prevented them from leaving the tent, that level of caution was warranted.

Haruhiro suspected this sound might be the cause of that mysterious phenomenon, but it might be the work of a relic, too.

Whether his guess was on the mark or not, it was best to assume anything could happen in the Leslie Camp, and to focus on finding another exit.

Haruhiro and the party had searched twelve rooms now. Thus far, they had all been about three square meters and separated from the others by deep purple curtains. There was always a side table and lamp.

There might, or might not, be other objects, too. However, there had yet to be a case with a variety of items in the same room.

The rooms with only a side table and lamp, let's call them empty rooms, had numbered seven. For the remaining five, the breakdown was as follows.

The Door Room, with a wooden door.

The Sculpture Room, with a statue of a nude, probably human, woman.

The Keyring Room, with a ring of keys left out on a chair.

The room they were in now was the second one with a box.

The box in the first such room had been similar to this box in terms of the size and material used, but a different color. The box in the first room had been a blackened gold, and this room's box was a copper-like color.

Shihoru hesitantly raised her hand.

"There's something bothering me..." she began, and then

showed them a note with a simple layout of each room. "The entrance we came in... this spot should have been on the outer edge of the tent, but..."

Haruhiro and the party had used the room with their entrance, and the two rooms to the left and right of it, as their starting point, and searched four rooms inwards from each of them, one after another.

"It may sound weird to say this, but I wonder what's outside the outer edge..." she went on.

Kuzaku cocked his head to the side. "There is nothing outside the outer edge, right? I mean, wouldn't that be outside?"

Setora crossed her arms and muttered to herself, "That's how it's supposed to be."

Kiichi was well-behaved, sitting there and looking up at Setora.

"Yeah," Merry agreed.

"How it would normally be..." Haruhiro murmured.

That's right. If it isn't like that, something's wrong.

Haruhiro tried returning to the Door Room, which was to the right of the entrance.

"Normally, the other side of this curtain would be outside... right?" he asked.

The Door Room had curtains on four sides, too. Of those four sides, the door in question was in front of the curtain in the direction that was straight ahead when entering this room from the door with the entrance.

Haruhiro was in front of the curtain that was on his right while facing the door.

The tent itself was a whitish color. If he drew back that deep purple curtain, there should have been a whitish outer curtain separating the inside from the outside. He wasn't fully conscious of it, but that was why he hadn't tried to go past here.

There was no way they could go past here.

"Wait, Haruhiro," Kuzaku said. "I'll handle this."

When Kuzaku went to touch the curtain, Kejiman let out a bizarre cry of "Zumoy!" and charged forward. He pulled the curtain back with gusto.

Kejiman called out, "Nnnnnnnnnnnnngh! Whaaaaaaaaaaaaa...?!"

He'd had a feeling—no, he'd been half-convinced—that this was a likely possibility, so Haruhiro wasn't all that surprised.

No, that was a lie. He was surprised, but more than that, he was confused about how to interpret this situation. Because it was there, after all.

Based on the tent's layout, he should have hit a curtain to the outside, or gone outside, one of the two, but there was a room with a side table, a lamp, and curtains each of the four directions, the one Kejiman now held open included.

It was a room.

There was a room.

An empty room.

"Uh, yeah, so basically..."

Haruhiro pretended to think about it. Or rather, he was trying to think, but he couldn't help but feel it was pointless. What did this mean?

"Heh heh!" Kejiman cackled. "Don't you get it?"

It seemed even Kejiman was in no hurry to enter that empty room, because he turned back to them while still holding the curtain open.

The man paused. "Well, I... I have no clue. What's going on here?! It's scary! Sca-ry! W-w-w-we'd better be able to get back home, damn it...!"

"Look, this is your fault to begin with..." Haruhiro muttered.

"You're my bodyguard, so do something about it, you ass!"

"Who is an ass?" Setora asked coldly. "Watch your mouth, you lowlife."

While Setora told him off, Kejiman started bawling. His nose was running pretty badly, too. "Forgive me, my queen. My goddess. But I had no idea it would end up like this..."

It would have been nice to have Kejiman spare a thought for those he had dragged into this mess, but there was zero chance that taking him to task over it would improve the situation.

Haruhiro wanted to, though. He wanted to really give him an earful.

This was a situation that required a little self-restraint. But he knew the trick to holding himself back.

This was better than the days he'd spent being tormented by that one idiot. If he thought of it that way, he could tolerate it, somehow.

But wait, was it, really...?

That was questionable. Kejiman was pretty awful, too.

"This may be another world... maybe," Merry said, then added, "That's just a possibility, though," as if making excuses.

"A-another world, huh?!" That might not be something to panic over, but for some reason, Haruhiro was. "Hmm, yeah, another world, huh? Makes sense. It's another world, huh? Another world..." he mumbled, his brain racing desperately.

In the end, what did it mean? Another world? What was that?

"Huh...?" he mumbled. "This place? Like the Dusk Realm, or Darunggar?"

"Another world..." Kejiman adjusted the bridge of his glasses with the middle finger of his right hand. "Can I go...?"

"Go." Setora pointed towards the ground with her index finger. "Go at once. Go, and never return."

"Sorryyyy! I was just joking around! That's not what I really want to ask! I was thinking, maybe you people have been to other worlds?! It sounded like you had, at least!"

"I have not, but Haru and the rest have," Setora said.

"Woooow! Awesoooooooooooooome!" Kejiman's eyes bulged out, and he did a little dance.

What was with this guy? Seriously. He was gross.

"Another world! How I've dreamed of going! I've always wanted to see one before I died! Oh! What if this really is another world?! Shouldn't I be happy?! My wish may have come true, right?!"

"How nice," Kuzaku said with a look of exasperation on his face.

But it's not that nice, though, okay? Haruhiro thought with annoyance.

"Relics, huh..." he muttered.

He didn't know much, but Haruhiro did have one. He'd gotten it from Soma. The receiver. It seemed to be broken, but—

Right. Now that he thought about it, he hadn't told his comrades yet. Oh, crap. He needed to say something. But, yeah, not now. This wasn't the time.

Anyway, if he remembered correctly, Soma's comrade, Shimam, had said something about this. The word "relic" was a general term for all things that couldn't be replicated with current technology, but had clearly been made in the past. Basically, it was a word for things that carried powers beyond human knowledge, which were of unknown origin and design.

Haruhiro wondered if they'd been hypnotized by that sound or something, and that was why they couldn't leave. Maybe there was a musical instrument-like relic somewhere in the tent with that sort of power. But it seemed possible that a relic was changing the inside of the tent, turning it into another world like Merry was saying. Or it was possible the entrance had led to another world, and this was a one-way trip.

None of it was more than speculation, though.

He felt like he was almost ready to give in to desperation. Maybe they should just do whatever at this point. Keep going, and going, and going. Eventually, they had to hit a dead end.

Haruhiro cleared his throat. He breathed out, letting the tension out of his shoulders. This wasn't a common situation, but was anyone at risk of dying right this second?

The answer was no. This wasn't a desperate situation.

So the first priority was to avoid falling into a life-or-death crisis. To that end, they would have to get out of the Leslie Camp.

He was afraid of acting carelessly out of desperation. It was important to be consistent. Keep doing the same work, without giving up. As long as he did that, this wasn't undoable, even for someone with no special talent like Haruhiro.

"What we need to do hasn't changed," he said. "Let's keep searching, one room at a time."

11 | **Never Saw It Coming**

IT'S NOT UNDOABLE.

Haruhiro had once believed that. Or more like tried to make himself believe it, maybe.

Twenty-three boxes, of varying size, shape, color, and constituent materials.

Seven books, laid out on pedestals.

Five statues, of varying design.

Three shelves, with drawers and stuff.

One door.

One ring of keys laid out on a chair.

One candle stand, likewise laid out on a chair.

Eight other things, not easily categorized.

And two hundred and fifteen empty rooms, each containing only a side table and a lamp.

That was the result of searching two hundred and sixty rooms.

Using the room with the entrance they couldn't go back out as a point of reference, the party had continued exploring the Leslie Camp. They were in the Entrance Room again now. They had slumped to the ground there, in fact.

In Kejiman's case, the moment he'd sat down on the carpet, he'd laid back and started snoring.

"How long do you figure it's been?" Kuzaku was sitting cross-legged, his back hunched, and his head hanging. There was no strength in his voice.

"I feel like... my sense of time has gotten fuzzy..." Shihoru murmured.

Shihoru was sitting back to back with Merry, and they were supporting each other.

Setora seemed relatively energetic. She had a notebook open, and was enthusiastically taking notes on the Leslie Camp. Kiichi was rolled up into a ball next to her, clearly sleepy.

"This is endless," Setora said briskly. "Is it time we investigated a relic? Or do we try opening that door?"

In fact, Haruhiro had been considering the same idea. After all, the only thing that it seemed like they could go in through or out of was that door. It was human nature to want to try opening it, an impulse that was too strong to resist. It was pretty hard to ignore that urge.

Haruhiro was also fighting the desire to open each of the boxes. The existence of the keyring stood out to him, and he wondered if maybe it was for opening the boxes. But, as far as he could see, none of those boxes had keyholes.

Did they even open? He hadn't tried yet. For now, maybe it would be okay to check whether they could open one of them or not? Was that no good?

Yeah, it was no good.

Wait, was it?

He didn't really know. His ability to make decisions was impaired. He was aware of that, so he couldn't do anything else. For now, he couldn't help but feel like everything he was thinking was mostly wrong, and the keyring bugged him.

The door. If they opened it, what would be there?

The boxes. Relics...

"We still have water..." Merry was rummaging through a container. "We're nearly out of food."

They had all left their large packs at the camp. Haruhiro only had the minimum of equipment he needed. He regretted that now. He'd never expected this to happen, though. He'd been careless.

"One thousand gold," Kuzaku said suddenly.

"Huh...?" Haruhiro looked over at Kuzaku. For an instant, their eyes met.

Kuzaku looked away. "...No. It's nothing. Forget it."

"Forget it...?" For several seconds, Haruhiro was in a daze.

Each platinum coin was thirty grams. There were a hundred of them. Three kilos. It was by no means an amount they couldn't carry, but that bag with a hundred platinum coins in it was heavier than its physical weight. The bag itself was made to last, and it was pretty bulky, so it wasn't all that light.

During their trip, Kuzaku had shouldered that impressive bag as they walked, and kept it close at hand as he slept. However, something was up.

Huh? Where's the bag? I don't see it, thought Haruhiro.

"Well, you know..." Haruhiro said. "These things happen, I guess?"

They'd just woken up. They weren't anywhere where it was likely to be stolen. Kuzaku must not have imagined they wouldn't be able to return.

Kuzaku sniffled, and with a depressed tone, which was so not like him, he mumbled, "...Sorry."

Haruhiro exchanged looks with Shihoru, who had an, *Oh...* look on her face.

It seemed Merry had picked up on the situation, and she looked anxiously at Kuzaku.

Setora was staring at her notebook, muttering something in a quiet voice.

Kiichi had apparently gone to sleep.

Kejiman's loud snoring was an annoyance.

Well, you know, Haruhiro thought with a sigh, *it's just money, right?*

It's a lot of money, though. Like, a ridiculous amount? It's not like it's gone. It's not like he lost it, to be precise. So long as we can get back, the thousand gold is in the place where we were camping. That's if we can get back.

Can we, or not? That's the problem now. This isn't the time to worry about money. If we can get back, that solves everything. It all comes after that.

116

The money doesn't matter. Forget it. Just forget it. No, the more I try to forget it, the harder it is to forget. I'm getting fixated on it.

Okay. Let's think about it this way. There was no money. We never had a thousand gold to begin with. It never existed.

Let's go with that. Yeah. I feel better... What a waste, damn it.

No, no. We'll go back. No matter what, we'll go back. Not for the money, but because we have to go back. We'll get out of the Leslie Camp. That's all that matters for now.

It was just making the best of a bad situation, but he managed to get himself fired up. Still, his head remained cool. He had to think calmly. Moving forward on momentum alone wasn't Haruhiro's style.

Even then, there was no question they had hit a dead end. If they just continued on as they were, it was plain to see that none of them would have the willpower to keep going.

Haruhiro stood up. "Let's investigate the door. It's right over there, thankfully."

It was in the next room, so it was really close.

Kejiman, who was still snoring loudly, didn't wake up when they called his name or when Setora kicked him, so they left him there.

The party moved over to the Door Room, and started scrutinizing the exterior of the door.

"The key..." Haruhiro crouched down and brought his face close to the doorknob. The door itself was wooden, but the knob and backplate were made of metal. The holes above and below the knob looked like nothing if not keyholes. "Never seen a door with two keyholes before..."

"Yeah. For sure." Kuzaku crouched next to Haruhiro. "Dunno if it's locked or not, though..."

It looked like he'd gotten back on his feet. Kuzaku wasn't the type to drag things with him, which was good because it meant he wasn't a pain to deal with.

"Yeah..." Haruhiro agreed. "I wonder. There's no way to tell, just from looking at it."

"Can you see the other side through the keyhole?"

"Why don't you try?"

"Can I?"

"It's all right. Just don't touch it."

"Okay. Just don't push me, all right?"

"I'd never do that..."

"It's just a cliché, you know." Kuzaku closed his left eye, and brought his right eye up close to the keyhole.

It was just for a moment, but Haruhiro felt a little like pushing him. Well, not that he would.

"How is it?" asked Setora.

"Nah. Can't see a thing." Kuzaku moved away from the door.

Of course he couldn't see anything. Keyholes and peepholes were two separate things.

Suddenly, Shihoru gulped. "The keys..."

"Yeah, I thought that, too." Haruhiro licked his lip.

There had been no keyholes on the boxes, or on the drawers of the shelves, either. But there were keyholes on this door. If it was locked, where were the keys?

There had been a ring of keys left out on a chair.

"I've got my tools, so I could use Picking on it," Haruhiro said. "Maybe it's not even locked, though..."

As he said that, he checked Merry's expression. Merry was looking at Haruhiro, but her mouth was slightly open, and she seemed a bit out of it. She must have been pretty exhausted. That had to be why.

Setora picked up Kiichi, who was rubbing against her leg.

The door. The keys. It feels like they we're being led into it, and I don't like that. Is that overthinking things? I think being overcautious is best, but this is going nowhere. No matter what, we're going to have to take a risk.

"Everyone, back away," he said.

He waited until his comrades retreated, then grabbed the doorknob.

He narrowed his eyes. He was relying on the sense of touch in his fingers and his hearing.

Once he decided to do it, there must be no hesitation. Indecision would play havoc with his senses.

The knob didn't turn.

No matter how much strength he put into it, it didn't budge. This feeling. Sound. It was locked. No doubt about it.

Haruhiro let go of the knob. He looked down, and sighed. He was sweating profusely. It was an awfully chilly sweat.

"It won't open," he said. "Let's go get the keys."

The Keyring Room was close. That didn't feel entirely unintentional.

Regardless, when they went to the Keyring Room, the ring

of keys was obviously still on top of the chair. The metal ring was blackish with hardly any luster, and there were keys in a variety of shapes, nine in total.

Picking it up and looking at it, it wasn't especially heavy. It was a normal keyring.

Haruhiro stood in front of the door, holding the keyring, while Kuzaku and the rest stood back.

"...Okay, let's test it," Haruhiro said.

There were nine keys. Two keyholes, one above and one below the knob.

Haruhiro picked a key at random, testing it in the upper keyhole first.

It slid in, without a sound.

The smoothness of it was bizarre. What was more, the key was tightly meshed within the locking mechanism. He probably couldn't pull it out.

He tried pulling on the key. It went as expected. Didn't budge an inch.

"...What is this?" he whispered despite himself.

It seemed his comrades didn't hear him.

Don't get agitated, Haruhiro told himself, breathing in, then out.

It wasn't just a keyring. Was that what this meant? Maybe the keyring was a relic, too. If so, what power did it harbor?

Haruhiro turned the key. It unlocked. He could tell from the noise it made.

That was when it happened.

The key went hazy, as if it was turning to smoke. While he was busy thinking that was impossible, it vanished without a trace.

Haruhiro had been holding the key. As it vanished, the keyring fell to the carpet with a clatter.

"Haru?" Setora called his name.

Haruhiro picked up the keyring, then gave a meaningless response. "...Uh, yeah."

He tried counting the keys.

Eight. There really were just eight of them. He was short one.

Haruhiro turned around and showed everyone the keyring. "When I opened the lock, it vanished."

"Huh?" Kuzaku asked. "Wait, but the keys are there..."

"No, it was just the key I used that vanished, and..." While he was explaining to Kuzaku, he was able to calm down a little. "Well, this is a relic. It's like, I dunno... the universal key? But one use only."

"Gimme!" Kejiman extended both hands like a bowl. "No! I demand it as your employer! I hired you, so ownership of that relic should belong to me! Now, give!"

"We refuse."

With that one short line from Setora, Kejiman started acting a lot more meekly. "I-It was a joke. Oh, gosh. You know I wasn't serious. Hee hee..."

Okay, maybe not meekly. Regardless, if things were as Haruhiro suspected, they could open any door eight more times. His Picking was influenced by experience, and he wasn't guaranteed to succeed. It took a fair amount of time, too. Furthermore, depending on the type of lock, there were times Picking was ineffective. Besides, anyone could use a universal key.

It was an exceptionally useful, but frightening, toll, depending on how you looked at it.

Haruhiro unlocked the lower lock with another one of the keys. The universal key he used vanished, as expected, leaving him with seven left.

Now the door ought to open.

"Would you let me open it?" Kuzaku volunteered.

He was probably concerned for Haruhiro's safety, but if there were traps or other mechanisms, Kuzaku would never notice them.

Haruhiro was about to refuse, but then Setora offered a counter proposal.

"Let's have our employer, Kejiman, open it. He is our employer, after all."

"Me?! N-no, but that's..."

"What? Was it all just bravado, then? What a boring man."

"I'm not a boring man, not me! No way! If anything, I'm so interesting that it's hard to keep up with me! I try to be a good customer, but so many serving girls at the tavern have rejected me! Okay, I'll do it!"

As soon as Kejiman finished rambling, he pushed Haruhiro aside, grabbed the knob, and gave it a good hard turn.

"Hey, whoa, not so fast!" Haruhiro cried.

"Will it be a demon lord?! Will it be an evil god?! Bring 'em on!" Kejiman opened the door.

Oh, so that's how it's gonna be, Haruhiro reflected.

"Wh-wh-wha...!" Kejiman bent backward in surprise. He practically did a bridge. In a way, it was impressive. "What is thiiiiiiiis?!"

Well, as galling as it was to agree with Kejiman, it wasn't hard to see why he wanted to shout out loud.

Beyond the door was a deep purple curtain.

What did this mean?

Nothing. The door had seemed to be positioned so meaningfully, so Haruhiro had been sure it was no ordinary fixture, but rather a special door.

And it wasn't. It was a plain door, like any other.

"Don't lock it, then." Kuzaku crouched down, and let out a sigh.

Setora put a hand on Kuzaku's shoulder. Then she stared at the hand, as if unsure it was in fact her own. She yanked it back at once.

"Well, you know..." Haruhiro sighed.

"It's a letdown... but nothing bad happened, so..." Shihoru let out a weak, awkward laugh.

Haruhiro hadn't done anything wrong, but he felt kind of sorry. Still, like Shihoru said, it was better to look at it positively. Even if that was awfully hard.

Merry was still looking past the door. Was she in a daze? That didn't seem to be it. Her expression was stiff. Sharp, even. There was a look in her eyes as if she was suspicious of something.

Haruhiro looked to the door, too. That was when it happened.

"Damn it alllllllllll!" Kejiman shouted.

Was he blowing off steam? It looked like he was going to tackle the curtain on the other side of the door.

Let him. Haruhiro didn't stop him.

And then...

Oh, so that's how it's gonna be.

"He..."

Haruhiro probably tried to say something. *"He"? "He" what?* What came next? What happened?

That was unclear.

"...He's gone?" Kuzaku said.

That was it. *He's gone.*

That was what Haruhiro had been trying to say.

"Where did he go...?" Setora whispered. She meant Kejiman, of course.

"He vanished." Merry seemed surprised. Her face was twitching.

Haruhiro, for some reason, felt a little relieved. No, now wasn't the time for relief.

He'd vanished. Kejiman had.

Shihoru's eyes went wide, and she shook her head repeatedly.

The door was still open. The curtain on the other side wasn't moving in the slightest. Kejiman had charged towards the curtain. But he hadn't just made contact. Just in front of it—he'd vanished?

"That's weird... right?" Kuzaku approached the door and stuck his right hand out.

"Hold on, wait!" Merry put forth, sounding a little worried.

But everything past Kuzaku's right elbow had vanished. "... Huh?"

"Wha—"

This time, Haruhiro knew what he had been trying to say. *"What's going on?"* But before he could, Haruhiro jumped and grabbed Kuzaku's right arm. He wrapped his arm around it, and tried to pull him back to this side.

"Owowowowow?! Ha-Haruhiro, I feel it on the other side, too..."

"Whaa?!" Haruhiro cried.

This was no good. He had his heels dug in, and he was pulling with all his might, but he couldn't pull him free.

Kuzaku was in pain, and panicking on top of that. "Oh, crap! Oh, crap! I feel something pulling on the other side, too!"

"H-hang in there!"

"No, I am! It's just, if I end up in there, I think..."

It was unclear what Kuzaku was thinking, but he stuck his left hand into the door. It vanished. Everything past Kuzaku's left wrist did.

It made no sense. But was this it? Looking at the situation, if he went inside the door, he'd vanish. Was that how it worked?

"I-It looks like I won't cease to exist! I-I can still feel! My right hand, it's being pulled from the other side, I mean! But once I go in, there may be no coming back here..."

"No way!" Haruhiro was speechless. Despite that, he kept pulling on Kuzaku.

"Dammit! Sorry, Haruhiro, everyone, looks like I've gotta go to the other side. You don't have to come with me. There's no knowing where it goes... I'm really sorry!"

Kuzaku's left arm, his left leg, and his right leg moved through the door. He was vanishing. Gradually. Kuzaku was. This was extremely bizarre.

"Uwah...!" Kuzaku cried.

He was being sucked in. Or rather, he was being pulled from the other side. Haruhiro was still holding on to him. Not to his right arm anymore. He had both arms around his torso from behind, and was holding on tight.

"Ha-Haruhiro, let go. I'll be fine. I'll manage somehow. This is pretty painful, too..."

"What're you smiling for, man?" Haruhiro cried.

"I mean, this is nothing to cry about."

"Yeah..." Haruhiro loosened his grip.

Kuzaku slipped through Haruhiro's arms.

It was over in an instant.

Kuzaku was swallowed up by the door.

"Haruhiro-kun..." Shihoru whispered.

Haruhiro didn't turn to look. "Sorry. I know we haven't talked it over... but I've already decided what to do."

Shihoru and Merry surely wouldn't object.

Nyaa, Kiichi meowed.

"Honestly..." Setora seemed exasperated, but also amused. "Being with you people is never boring."

Grimgar of Fantasy and Ash

12 | Paranoia

NOT ALL beginnings are the same.

For instance, there could be a beginning like this.

When they passed through the door, there was wind blowing beyond it, and something about the air was plainly different.

"...It's sweet," Haruhiro murmured.

Was it the taste? The fragrance? Who knew. Whatever it was, it was slightly sweet.

The light was bright, but not brilliantly so.

The scenery was bizarre.

The ground was white. Was it sand? The grains were varying sizes, and more jagged than smooth. There were plants of some sort growing to a height of three to four meters. They were a bright pink, so maybe they were actually coral.

This was land, though. They could breathe fine, so it was probably land.

The sky was milky white, with a little blue here and there.

Like polka dots. Those lights scattered through the sky, could they be stars, maybe? Even though it was midday? Or was it night? There was no sun to be seen. It was bright, though, so it was probably the middle of the day.

Kejiman was holding on to Kuzaku, who had fallen to the white ground.

"Haruhiro..." Kuzaku said.

"It was you..." Haruhiro pressed his palm against his forehead.

Obviously, he wasn't talking about Kuzaku. Kuzaku had been pulled to the other side. Who had been responsible for that? He'd had a sneaking suspicion, but now he was sure of it.

"I-It's not like I was, uh..." Kuzaku began awkwardly.

Kejiman didn't just not let go of Kuzaku; he clung to him. "Look... I-I was lonely, okay? Me, being out here, all by my lonesome? That's not funny. You understand, right? What would you have done if I died?!"

"Come on... Don't cry while clinging to me. You're smothering me here. Like, this is gross."

"Don't call it gross! We're tight, you and me, Kuzaku-kun!"

"There's nothing between us. Now stop it, I'm serious..."

It wasn't long before Setora and Kiichi, Shihoru, and Merry came through, appearing at their side in that order.

"This is..." Shihoru took labored breaths, looking around cautiously.

Setora's expression was no different from usual for her, but seeing the way she held Kiichi tight, she must have been a little worried.

Merry's eyes were downcast, her lips drawn taut, as if she were trying to remember something.

Setora scrunched up her nose. "Something smells sweet."

Haruhiro nodded. This sweet-smelling air, it was kind of gross.

"Ah..." Shihoru pointed up. "That thing... it's getting bigger?"

"Whoa! Biehhhhhhhhhhhhhhhhhhhhhhhh!" Kejiman started screaming while still holding on to Kuzaku.

Kuzaku started making a fuss, too. "Huh? Huh? Huh? What? What is that? What is that?! Wh-wh-wh-whaaaa?!"

"Stars...?" Merry whispered.

"Shooting stars?" Setora was still relatively calm, but maybe she should have been a bit more panicked in this situation.

One of the bright shining points in the polka dot sky was changing size with each moment that passed.

If it were shrinking, it would become invisible, and that might be the end of it. But it was growing. This couldn't be ignored.

That star-like thing was getting closer to the ground. Falling. The star was falling. Probably at a very high speed.

"Re..." Haruhiro began to say, *Retreat!* But then he hesitated.

The star was already the size of a person's head. It looked like it might be falling straight towards the party, too. Even if they tried to run, it would be pointless, wouldn't it? Even as they panicked, the star had doubled and then doubled again in size, continuing to grow quickly. It wasn't really growing, though.

"Sh... Shouldn't we run...?" Shihoru's suggestion brought Haruhiro back to his senses.

That was right. It would be one thing if he was alone, but his comrades were here. How could he give up so easily?

"Run, but don't get split up! Come on, I said run!"

Haruhiro kicked Kejiman, who was still not letting Kuzaku go, in the butt.

"Hhhhhh?!"

Kejiman took off like he'd been shot out of a cannon, and Kuzaku, who was now free, took off running, too. Setora and Kiichi took off as well, and Merry and Shihoru followed them, practically hand in hand. Haruhiro brought up the rear.

Turning back, the star had gotten so massive that it was hard to compare it to anything. Was anything else this large? How far away was it? Like a few hundred meters overhead? But it was a bit strange. Weren't shooting stars usually on fire? Like, from the friction? There was no sign of that here. It wasn't hot, either. Nor did it make any sound. It was just getting closer.

This might be the first, and last, time he would ever see an object so massive and sparkling. If it hadn't been falling in his direction, he'd have stared at it. It was incredible. It was no particular color, just brilliance filling his entire field of vision and, oh, was it ever something.

"Everyone—" He managed to get that much out, but everything else after it was an incoherent scream, intermixed with the voices of his own comrades.

They were being crushed. He felt something like pressure on his whole body.

It's over, he thought. But the fact he could think that at all meant it was not, in fact, over.

Bannnnnnnnnnnnnnnnnnnnnnnnnnnnnng! Something popped. Haruhiro was thrown through the air and then rolled. His whole face got covered in sand. His eyes stung. He couldn't see. Not a thing. His ears were messed up, too.

It looked like he hadn't been crushed. He was alive. What had that been, just now?

Haruhiro brushed the sand off as he got up. "Kuzaku! Shihoru! Merry! Setora! You okay...?!"

His own voice sounded so distorted, so far away.

"I-I'm okay!" Kuzaku shouted. "Where is everyone?! I can't see!"

"I'm okay!" Shihoru called. "Merry's here, too..."

"Yeah, we made it, somehow..." Merry agreed.

"What was that?! Kiichi?!" Setora yelled.

"Nyaa!"

"I-I'm alive?! By some miracle?! Life is woooonderful!" Kejiman screamed.

It looked like everyone was intact, including one extra they could really have done without.

Haruhiro blinked and rubbed his eyes, waiting for his vision to recover.

It was blurry, but he could see. His vision was getting clearer. "This is..."

There was something resembling snow falling. When it touched the palm of his hand, it instantly vanished.

It wasn't cold. That ruled out it being snow. What could it be? It resembled something.

Kuzaku reached out with his long arm, catching several of them at the same time.

"...What are these? They're almost like little soap bubbles."

"Yeah, now that you mention it..." Haruhiro looked up at the polka dot sky once more.

It might be that the infinite minuscule bubble-like objects now raining down were fragments of the fallen star. That must have meant it wasn't a star at all. Then what was it? Haruhiro couldn't possibly know. He let out a sigh.

"Let's just be glad we're not dead for—"

"Augh?!"

The scream that cut him off came from Kejiman, so for a moment Haruhiro didn't want to look, but that wasn't an option.

Turning in the direction of the voice, Kejiman was collapsed in front of a thicket made from some pink-colored coral or plant. Was this him acting weird again, like always? No.

That wasn't it. Not this time.

"H-h-h-h-h-help me...!" Kejiman was being dragged towards the thicket.

"Eek!" Shihoru screamed.

Inside the thicket, there was something there.

"Oh, come on..." Kuzaku seemed more exasperated than frightened, and Haruhiro felt the same.

Was it a spider? Inside the thicket, there was something like a massive spider. But it was only *like* a spider, and—

Hold on, that thing clearly wasn't a spider. Its legs weren't spider legs. They were like octopus legs. Wasn't it an octopus, then? He couldn't call it that, either. Its overall form more closely resembled a spider, after all. But the head was neither spider nor octopus.

The face wasn't just pale, it was pure white, with the whites of its eyes being black, and the pupils being golden. It didn't seem male or female, but it was the head of a bald-headed human.

Kejiman had been caught by its legs. He let out mysterious cries like, "Afwaih?!" as it dragged him into the thicket.

What was happening? He couldn't see Kejiman anymore, or hear his voice.

The monster was still in the thicket. Its mouth flapped open and closed as it stared in his direction with those disconcerting eyes.

Haruhiro bent his knees and leaned forward. He was ready to run, but Kejiman was their employer. Besides, Haruhiro was no monster. He had to help him.

He tried to step forward.

In that instant, the creature began retreating. With its octopus-like legs wriggling, it backed away at an incredible speed.

"Haru!"

Was that Merry, or Setora? Or had both of them called him? It was hard to tell immediately.

Haruhiro drew his dagger.

The ground.

From out of the sand, a dark black thing, probably a hand, flew towards him.

If Haruhiro hadn't pulled his right foot up fast, that black hand-like thing would have caught him by the ankle.

The black hand-like thing, or its main body rather, started crawling up out of the ground.

Haruhiro jumped back.

Was it human? Whatever it was, it was black. It wasn't just a hand. Its shoulders, head, neck, chest, and torso were all black.

It did not, however, have legs. In their place, it had something resembling a sea anemone growing out of it. Its head lacked eyes or a nose, and was split vertically. Was that its mouth, maybe? It was lined with thin, thorn-like teeth. Its body was black all over, but the inside of its oral cavity was yellow. It was a bright lemon yellow.

That sea anemone jerk with the dark, grotesque upper torso wasn't alone. Others started to come out from all over the place. Lots of them.

Were Haruhiro's comrades safe? At a glance, none of them appeared to have been caught. For now, at least.

"What are these things?!" Kuzaku exclaimed.

The guy drew and swung his large katana, and the sea anemone jerk with the dark, grotesque upper torso—you know what, that was too long, maybe just grotesque jerk was good enough—got one of its arms lopped off.

Were Merry and Setora fighting back, too? How about Shihoru? Haruhiro wanted to look, but couldn't afford to. He had a number of those grotesque jerks crawling towards him.

Haruhiro danced around to avoid their grasping hands and biting heads. Naturally, he didn't feel like dancing at all.

He wasn't a good dancer, and he didn't like it. He was just desperately dodging, and as a result, he ended up pulling off some pretty complicated dance steps. But man, this was crazy. Real crazy.

"The thickets...!" Haruhiro shouted. He was trying to caution his comrades to be careful of the thickets, but that was all he ended up getting out.

There were thickets of that pink coral-like plant stuff all around. It was fair to say they were surrounded by thickets. There was one just behind Haruhiro, and just as he was thinking it was suspicious, another strange creature sprang out of it, just as he should've expected.

"Wah...!" he shouted.

It was a centipede. Only huge. It had to be the size of a human baby. On top of that, its unpleasantly white legs looked like human arms. It had a lot of those appendages, and when they were all moving it looked kinda scary.

No, not just kinda. It was pretty scary.

Haruhiro missed his chance to dodge, and it knocked him down. Its twenty to thirty legs with their little hands were squirming. Because they were small, they didn't do any harm other than creeping him out, but he couldn't fight the feeling of revulsion that welled up from inside him.

"Oh, geez!" Haruhiro immediately shoved it off him.

When he did, though he wasn't trying to look, and would rather not have, he saw the underside of that thing. The upper side had seemed to have a carapace, and it was kind of like a centipede, which was unsettling enough, but the underside was all bumpy. Like fish eggs, if he were to make a comparison.

Yes, like eggs. Were those eggs? Was it incubating them? Would they hatch? Were there going to be more of those things?

"Dammit!"

Haruhiro jumped up. He couldn't take it.

This was crazy. Not any one thing in particular; it was all totally abnormal.

The pink coral or plant or whatever it was, the human-octopus-spider thing, the grotesque jerks, the incubator centipede, the star that had fallen, the polka dot sky, those things flying through that sky now—

What? What were they? Birds? No, that wasn't it. They were too long to be birds. Way too long. They were like flying intestines. If an intestine sprouted several pairs of wings. Was that possible? It wasn't impossible, right?

It could well be that Haruhiro had gone quite insane. This was bizarre, after all. Bizarre, and incoherent. It wasn't like this was a dream. It was a nightmare, if anything.

Haruhiro relied almost purely on his reflexes to bat away the incubator centipede, then to kick away a grotesque jerk.

He needed to think less about himself and more about his comrades, the girls in particular. More than think, he had to act. He knew that. In his head.

"If we stay here...!" Merry began.

She must have been trying to say they'd be in trouble. It was a bad idea to stay here. That might be true. They should move.

But if they didn't move together, they'd be split up. He wanted to avoid that, so maybe it was better not to move? But if they stayed here and tried to keep dealing with the grotesque jerks and incubator centipedes, could they get out of this?

"Urkh?!" he squealed.

Something wrapped around his left ankle. An octopus. It was an octopus-like leg. The human-octopus-spider, huh?

It pulled him down before he could shout, *Oh, crap!*

He couldn't stay on his back. He flipped over. He got on the thing's belly, and stabbed his dagger into the ground.

No luck, huh? It didn't stop.

His dagger drew a line in the white ground. The line grew longer as he watched. He was being pulled at an incredible speed.

"Hahhhh!" Kuzaku shouted.

If Kuzaku hadn't rushed over, and cut off its octopus-like leg with a flash of his large katana, Haruhiro would have gone through the same thing as with the centipede.

"Get up!" Kuzaku grabbed his wrist and pulled him up.

There was no time to say thanks. The grotesque jerks were creeping towards them, one after another. The incubator centipede jumped at them, too, the human-octopus-spider reached out with its octopus leg, and the winged intestines even started to dive and hit them.

Haruhiro elbowed the incubator centipede, kicked the grotesque jerks, and slashed the winged intestines with his dagger. It felt squishy as he tore through the intestine, and the multicolored substance inside it that was neither quite fluid nor solid splattered.

Those contents were steaming. Not warm, but hot.

There were fist-sized—no, smaller than that—creatures hopping up and down. Frogs? Their bodies were blue, red, and yellow on the outside, with black or green stripes. But why did they have heads like a human baby's? With hair, even! Lots of it. Scary.

When he got tripped by a grotesque jerk and fell, another strange creature came out of the sandy ground right next to him. Looking at it, he didn't see eyes, and it was furry, so it was kind of like a mole. But when it opened its mouth, it was split like a starfish's, and there was an eyeball deep inside.

"Eek!" Haruhiro let out a scream despite himself, and tried to get up, but a number of incubator centipedes swarmed over him, and the bumpy bumps on their underside, those bumpy, egg-like bumps, were bumpy, so bumpy, nothing but bumpy, bumpy, bumps, that they were too bumpy, nothing could be so bumpy.

"Whaaaaaaaaaaaaaaaaaaahhhhhh?!"

Nope. He couldn't take any more of this. What did he mean? He didn't know, but he couldn't take any more of this. The bumps were too much. The bumpy bumpiness of all those bumps was one thing he couldn't stand.

Haruhiro was thrashing around. Not just his arms or his legs—his whole body was flailing as he went totally wild.

He wanted to flee. From this reality. No, from the bumps. He didn't want those bumps to be real.

How many of those incubator centipedes were there? How many bumps?

This was a dream. Yeah. It had to be a bad dream.

He felt like he was about to pass out. He wished he could. If he did, surely he'd return to reality.

He was ready to say, *I'm home,* and he just wanted to hear, *Welcome back* in response. He didn't care who from. He'd take it from anything, so long as it wasn't bumpy.

There was something wrapped around his left ankle. The octopus? Was it the octopus leg? He couldn't see, so he couldn't tell, because of the incubator centipedes and their bumps. Basically, those bumps, those damn bumps were to blame for all of this. Damn it, those damn bumps were just bumps.

"Obuhobuhobuh!" Haruhiro shouted as he somehow managed to kick free from that octopus leg or whatever it was. He felt like he was finished in a lot of ways, but if he let it keep dragging him, he'd be done for real.

"No, it's me, Haruhiro, me!"

He couldn't see because of all the bumps, but he could hear. That was Kuzaku's voice. Was Kuzaku trying to drag Haruhiro as he fled? Or was some monster imitating Kuzaku's voice and trying to take him away? Either was possible.

Whatever the case, there were bumps. Maybe the bumps had nothing to do with this. No, of course they had something to do with this. They were bumpy. If those nightmarish bumps were really just a dream, was it more likely to be Kuzaku, or a monster?

If it was a monster, he was finished. But somehow he couldn't find the will to resist. This had to be the bumps' fault.

Haruhiro quietly let himself get dragged.

Wah, hiah, kwah, oh, eah, gwana, nia, zwahh! The incubator centipede's bumps were emitting voice-like sounds. Each was a small sound, but there were many bumps, and it was like having some thousands of nonsensical whispers in his ear, which was really frightening. They were bumps, after all. The bumps were unbearable in their bumpiness.

Maybe I never knew fear before now, Haruhiro couldn't help but think. *Is this what scary is? Bumps, basically? Well, whatever, I don't care, I want away from these bumps. Seriously, spare me. No more bumps. This is crazy. If I could, I'd want to pull my brain out of my skull. Then, even if it was just my brain, I'd get it out of here.*

Suddenly the monster, or Kuzaku, or whatever it was, let go of his left ankle.

Haruhiro was no longer being dragged, but the incubator centipede, the bumps, they were still... what?

Still what? Scary. Help me.

"Haruhiro! Just wait! Now!"

Yeah.

I'm waiting.

Haruhiro was summoning every last ounce of his power in order to hold still.

The bumps were peeled away from Haruhiro's body one after another. The bumps attached to his face were removed first, so he felt better quickly.

Naturally, it wasn't any monster that had saved Haruhiro. It was Kuzaku.

Kuzaku didn't just leave the bumpy things alone—no, the incubator centipedes—he pulled them off Haruhiro, and then threw them at the nearby coral-like, plant-like things, stomped on them, and for the ones that kept moving afterwards, he stabbed them with his large katana.

With incredible speed, the incubator centipedes were all gone from Haruhiro.

If not for Kuzaku, who knew what would have happened? The incubator centipedes got together to hold Haruhiro down for some reason, but then did nothing more than press the bumps on their underside against him, making him hear those voices or sounds or whatever they were. That alone would have eventually been enough to drive him crazy, though. He was already feeling a little off in the head, and couldn't cast aside the doubt he'd gone pretty weird.

Kuzaku was his savior. He was thankful. So damn thankful. How could he express this gratitude? No matter how he did, it wouldn't be enough.

"Haruhiro!" Kuzaku jumped at him with his face twisted like some sort of demon. He hugged him tight. "You're okay, right?! Haruhiro! Haruhiro! Haruhiro?!"

Haruhiro nodded. Or he tried to, at least, but who knew? Was he managing to nod? It felt like his jaw was moving up and down a bit. In no time, his vision blurred.

"Haruhiro?! Hold on?! Why're you crying?! Are you hurt bad somewhere?!"

That wasn't it. He wasn't hurt bad enough anywhere to make him cry, but the tears wouldn't stop overflowing. Haruhiro rubbed his eyes. His hand was shaking. Was he in a state of shock? His whole body felt weak.

"...Everyone?" he whispered.

"Oh! That's right! Haruhiro, can you stand?!"

With help from Kuzaku, Haruhiro mobilized every last ounce of vital energy in his body to stand. His body felt kind of numb. His legs were trembling. His head was dizzy, and the tears still wouldn't stop. On top of that, his eyes wouldn't open. He felt extremely gross.

Shihoru.

Merry.

Setora.

And Kiichi. Where were they?

"Uh-oh, we're pretty far apart!" Kuzaku shouted.

It seemed Kuzaku had a rough grasp of where their comrades were. Haruhiro didn't know.

What is this? It hurts. Weird. I can't breathe right. It's like the air won't come in. My heart's beating like crazy. Am I going to die? No, no, now isn't the time. I can't afford to die.

He managed to force out, "Go... Kuzaku... go... g-get Shihoru... and the others..."

"No, but Haruhiro, you're kinda..."

"Go! Hurry! I'll go, too!"

"Then come with me! You have to stick with me, got it?!"

Kuzaku took off running. Haruhiro tried to follow. But he couldn't run. He couldn't breathe properly, either. His legs were unsteady, and walking was difficult.

For now, breathe, he told himself. *If I don't breathe in, I can't breathe out. So breathe in.*

Breathe in.

Breathe in.

It's sweet. Ohh...

How can it be so sweet?

He had to move forward. What about Kuzaku? Where was he? He didn't know.

His dagger. Where was his dagger? There. He'd dropped it.

He picked it up, and then what, was he moving forward? He didn't think he'd stopped.

He ended up in a thicket, or bushes of some kind, pushing through this pink, coral-like stuff, and there were creatures, monsters, whatever they were, things that moved were jumping at him, so he brushed them aside, shook them off, moving forward one step, or a half step, at a time.

Still, it was sweet.

It's sweet, too sweet, and now I'm getting sleepy.

He wanted to sleep so badly.

I can't. What would happen if I slept? I have to keep moving forward. Where to? What am I even moving forward for? So sleepy. What am I doing? It's sweet. Man, it's sweet. I'm tired.

At some point, he ended up on his belly. He had to get up.

Oh, but I'm so slee—

I can't see that man's face.

I don't know his face, but he's probably a man, I think.

He's built like a man.

I am behind that man.

Over his shoulder, I watch everything the man does.

Is it dark there? It's not bright. But it's not totally dark, either. It's kind of, I don't know, a sepia tone. Maybe the lighting makes it look that way.

The man walks.

His footfalls make no sound, as if he were using Sneaking.

He wears an old, fluffy coat-like garment, and he's a fairly large guy.

In his right hand, which is covered by a woolen mitten, he holds something.

A blade.

It looks like a carving knife. That, or a butcher's cleaver.

We're inside a house, I realize. It's a familiar house.

The man walks inside with his dirty shoes still on. Ignoring the door on our right, the door on our left, and the door further down on the right, he approaches the door at the end of the hall.

Is this his house, maybe?

No, I have the feeling it isn't... but I've seen it before.

This house, I know it.

The man, he opens the door.

Even when he does, the man makes hardly a sound.

The man is cautious, and more than anything, he's experienced.

When the door opens, I hear sounds.

Warm sounds.

Chop, chop, chop! Something is being cut up, likely vegetables. Yes, that's right, with a knife.

This room has an interconnected kitchen, living room, and dining room.

In the living room, there's a well-used sofa, a table that becomes a kotatsu in the winter, a TV, a TV stand, and a cabinet.

There are figures of characters, and bowls with images printed in them left here and there, and a number of photos on display. Those photos, none of them are new.

In the dining room is the dining room table and four chairs. A cupboard. It's not a big room. If anything, it's painfully small. The flowers in the small vase in the corner of the dining room table are not fresh, they're dried flowers. Poinsettias, if I recall.

The kitchen faces onto the dining room, and a woman wearing an apron is cooking. Preparing a late dinner, probably.

The woman hasn't noticed the man yet.

Hurry.

Notice.

Hurry.

This is bad. If you don't hurry up and notice, something terrible will happen.

I want to warn her. I would if I could. But I can't. I can only watch.

The woman's hand on the knife stops. She lays down the knife, and turns away.

She opens the refrigerator. Takes out something. She lays it on the food preparation area, and though I can't see it from here, she must have a pot on the element, and she takes the lid off it.

The woman finally realizes something. As if thinking, *Oh, is someone here?*

The man has already entered the dining room.

Seeing him, the woman raises her voice. "Ah!" The woman is shocked, and frightened. Well, of course.

The man is awfully big, he's a giant, and though I haven't seen his face, I doubt it's pretty. He must be hideous.

Besides, the man has a butcher's knife in his hands. He's not just holding it, but keeping it a chest level, ready to use at any time.

"Nooo, noooooo, stoooooop!" the woman screams.

Backing away, she runs into the shelf behind her, causing the rice cooker, mixer, and coffee maker to shake.

The man is unbothered by this, and he invades the kitchen. The rice cooker, mixer, and coffee maker get caught on the woman's arm, falling over as she flees.

In no time, she is cornered in the deepest point of the kitchen, next to the refrigerator.

The man does horrible things to the woman who is sitting on the floor, her back pressed up against the wall.

First, he uses the butcher's knife to — the woman's —. Next, he — to her —, and then he ties the woman's — which he — around his neck.

Still, the woman is breathing. Why is that, you might ask? But the man was careful with his work to make sure she didn't expire.

Each time the woman screams, the man goes, *Shhh, shhh!* as if silencing her.

Quiet.

Quiet.

Be quiet.

If you're noisy, it makes my work harder.

You understand, right? Pipe down. Don't make a racket.

From the woman's perspective, she has no reason to listen to the man, and she could probably stand to defy him, but each time, *Shh, shh!* Those vile, abrasive sounds come from between the man's teeth, she obediently shuts her mouth, and nods her head.

He does this cruel thing, puts her in incredible pain, making her scream because she can't hold it in, but when he silences her with his, *shh, shh,* the woman obeys him, as if that were her nature. Like a machine, created to always respond in a fixed way to a certain signal.

Many times the woman closes her mouth, nodding, and eventually, whether from pain or blood loss, she finally faints. When she does, the man's work is done at last. Immediately, he stabs her once through the heart, ensuring she will never wake again.

What in the world is with him? Who exactly is this man? It's hard to see him as a person. Not just because of what he's done. With his woolen mittens, his butcher's knife, and especially his muscular upper body, with biceps that are unnaturally swollen, and a chest which is too thick, there's something strange about him.

I don't know the man's face. That's suspicious, and strange.

I feel sick.

How could he kill her?

Yes, I know this woman. The woman who, though I wouldn't say she's unrecognizable now, has been broken into a lot of parts, and is lying in a lake of blood, other fluids, some sort of jelly-like substance, and a collection of squishy bits.

I know her as well as I know this house.

The man killed her.

Was that not enough for him?

The man wipes the blade of his butcher's knife on the hem of his soaked coat, and leaves the kitchen. He walks like before, his footfalls making no sound. Despite that, the man is humming.

It's a song, one I've heard somewhere before.

I've heard it once, or perhaps many times before, a long time ago, somewhere else that isn't here.

I don't know the title, and I hardly recall the lyrics. Maybe it was a hit a long time ago. It could have been a popular song. Whatever the case, the chorus is stuck in my head, and I can't get it out.

The man repeats the chorus again and again, humming to himself, as he returns from the dining room to the living room, and then passes through the open door to proceed down the hallway.

The man stops.

He slowly, quietly opens the door on our right. Blood sticks to the doorknob.

The room is dark. There's a bed. There's a mirror stand. There's a bookshelf. It's a bedroom. No one is here.

The man closes the door slightly, but not fully, leaving it that way as he keeps walking.

...No.

There's another door ahead on the right.

...Not there.

This hall.

That living room, dining room, and kitchen.

I know this room.

The man stops humming and reaches for the doorknob.

...Stop.

He turns the doorknob.

...Stop it, please.

There's a click, and the knob stops turning. The man slowly opened the door.

The lights are on. There aren't many things, but it's not pretty. There's just a closet, desk, chair, and bed for furniture, with towels, clothes, scraps of paper, and notebooks scattered around at random. No one comes into this room but family, or rather her mother, the lady the man just killed.

"My mom's always nagging me to clean up," she once said when I came here before, to return something I'd borrowed.

"Well, yeah, looking at it, I can understand," I remember having answered.

"You're saying it's dirty?" she asked.

"No, I wouldn't say that."

"You're thinking it, though."

"Yeah, just a little."

"It cleans up quick," she said, quickly moving the many things off to the side, piling them in the corner of the room.

When she did that, if I just ignored that one corner, it wasn't impossible to say it looked clean.

"I can do it if I try," she said, sounding a little proud.

It was so funny, I couldn't help but laugh.

That made her mad. "What?" she said, and punched me in the shoulder. Just lightly, though.

That's her, lying in bed, curled up a little.

Her eyes, they're not closed.

She's not sleeping, but she still hasn't noticed the unfamiliar man creeping into her room.

That because she's wearing noise-canceling earphones as she watches videos on her smartphone.

Stop it. Please.

The man silently creeps towards her.

I can hear the sound leaking from her earphones, though just faintly.

Finally, it seems the man, or probably his leg, has entered her sight, because she gulps and her whole body trembles. Pulling the earphone out of her right ear, she seems to jump straight up. Her eyes go wide, and she looks at the man.

"What?!"

Then, I think she was probably about to let out a high-pitched scream, but the man reaches out with his left hand, the hand wearing a mitten soaked in the blood of her mother, and he covers her mouth.

The man has big hands. Mittens big enough to fit those hands are probably hard to buy, so maybe it's handwoven. That's why it covers her mouth so easily.

The bloodstained mitten on the man's left hand fits snugly over the lower half of her face. When compared to the man's hand, her head is much too small. Thanks to that, she seems fake. Her head looks like a toy.

...Stop.

If the mood took him, and the man decided to crush her head, it probably wouldn't be impossible for him to do it.

He could do it, I think.

...No.

She's screaming something, and crying.

Shh, shh! The man shushes her like before.

Unlike her mother, however, she does not stop screaming.

It's easy to imagine what the man is about to do. I want to stop him. To cling to him, to beg, to make the man reconsider.

Please. I'm begging you. Please.

That's Choco.

Choco uses both arms to try and tear the man's left hand off her, but it doesn't budge. The man is very strong.

No...

No.

No.

No.

Shh, shh, the man orders Choco to silence herself, to be quiet, raising the butcher's knife, and swinging it down.

Into Choco's left shoulder the butcher's knife goes. Almost as if it was welcoming it. Like it was saying, *Please, come inside me, as deep as you like. It's okay to come in.*

The man's butcher's knife easily cleaves through Choco's clothes, her skin, her flesh, and even her collarbone. Deeply, and without restraint, it enters her.

Choco's cries become louder, more frantic. The man smothers them, though not perfectly, with his left hand and its blood-stained mitten.

It hurts, it hurts, it hurts! Choco is shouting.

Stop.

Stop.

Stop.

Stop.

The man turns his head to the side.

He won't stop.

He won't stop.

He won't stop.

He won't stop.

No way will he stop.

Shh, shh! The man lets out that harsh sound, pulling the knife out of Choco temporarily. This time he takes a horizontal swing, slamming it into Choco's side.

Choco screams and howls in pain.

When he pulls the butcher's knife free again, the wound is open, and from inside something, it looks like a hose, her entrails, pour out. From the wound in Choco's left shoulder, there's a spray of blood. Choco's eyes, they're halfway rolled back into her head.

Shh, shh! the man shushes her. This time he isn't telling her to be silent. *Hey, hey, don't pass out, not yet, I'm not done, hang in there,* he's encouraging her. More. There's more to come. The man pulls the butcher's knife out of Choco, then stabs it into her. Meanwhile, the man's mittened hand covers her mouth the whole time, holding her head and keeping her in place.

If he doesn't, it's not clear that Choco's still conscious at this point, but at the very least, she'd slump over, collapsing on the bed stained with her blood, entrails, and their contents. In order to prevent that, the man holds his prey, like he might hold up an anglerfish to fillet it, supporting Choco with just his left hand.

Keeping her suspended, he cuts up his prey, Choco, sometimes shaving off a piece of flesh, and wounding her however he likes. This is worse than defiling her.

You're not human. You monster. How could you do this?

Stop. Stop it.

But it's too late. Much too late.

Choco's already...

Who are you?

What are you?

The man turns.

At last, I see his face.

The man, his identity is...

Me.

The man has the same face as me.

13 | Another Way

"**U**NGH..."

With a shock like he'd been punched in the head—no, like he'd fallen from a high place and hit his body all over— Haruhiro awakened.

Had he been sleeping? Yes, he had been lying asleep on the white sand.

He felt like he'd seen some sort of dream.

It hadn't been a good dream. In fact, it had been a horrible nightmare.

He couldn't remember anything from it. Or rather, it looked like he had more important things to think about than some dream.

There was someone's foot right in front of Haruhiro's nose where he lay in the sand. That person was wearing long boots, and something resembling a raincoat. It might have been a red raincoat originally, but it was filthy, creating a pattern of light brown and dark brown spots. The overall color was a dark red.

The person held what looked like a shovel. It had a longish handle, with a scoop-like blade on the end. It was kind of dark in color, and had dents all over, but taken as a whole it was almost certainly a shovel.

"Kuh!" That person was swinging the shovel with incredible vigor.

Bam! The raincoated person knocked something back.

"Ah..." Haruhiro said, meaninglessly.

The sharp glance that came his way stabbed into him. "Move it!"

Raincoat wore their hood low over their eyes, and had a black cloth or something wrapped around the lower half of their face. It made it nearly impossible to tell what they looked like. However, from the voice, though not necessarily the way they spoke, and the not-exactly-muscular body, Haruhiro thought, *Maybe it's a woman.*

Whatever the case, it was best to do what Raincoat said for now.

Raincoat wasn't standing there alone.

There was a big man in front of Raincoat, a large man towering over her.

"No way." For a moment, Haruhiro's mind went blank.

The man wore a coat no less dirty than Raincoat's, with woolen mittens on his hands, and was holding a clearly dangerous-looking butcher knife. That butcher knife was now swinging violently towards Raincoat.

Haruhiro jumped up, almost in a daze.

"Kuh!" Raincoat knocked the man's butcher knife away with her shovel.

Haruhiro backed away one, then two steps, shocked and amazed. It was a wonder she could deflect that. After all, that guy, he was probably bigger than Kuzaku.

It wasn't so much his height that was amazing, as how thick his upper body, chest, shoulders, and arms were. Normally, humans couldn't get like that, no matter how they trained. He was clearly off the charts, out of the realm of what was normal, or even possible.

In which case, was he was just humanoid, and not actually human?

There was a reason Haruhiro couldn't accept that, and it bothered him.

The man's face.

He couldn't believe it, and didn't want to. But if Haruhiro's vision or memory hadn't failed him, he recognized that horrible giant of a man.

He knew him well. Intimately, you could say.

"...Why is he me?" Haruhiro whispered.

He had no hair. He was bald. He had no eyebrows, and was deathly pale. That was why they gave off a different impression at first glance, but no matter how many times Haruhiro looked at the shape of those facial features, they were his own.

"That because...!" Raincoat moved up while shouting. She swung her shovel up diagonally. She was fast. "...of the dream you saw, obviously!"

The giant man with Haruhiro's face may have been caught by

surprise, because he couldn't dodge quickly enough, and tried to block the shovel with his left arm.

However, he couldn't block it. The giant man's left arm was cut clean off a little below the elbow.

Was it something... that could cut like that? The blade of a shovel? If you sharpened it like crazy, it could... maybe?

The giant man's left arm fell to the sandy ground. His mittened left hand was wriggling. The blood coming from the point where it severed was properly red.

The giant man backed away.

Raincoat held her shovel at the ready, turning just her face towards Haruhiro. "That guy's clearly a dream monster you created. You have one hell of an id."

"I have no clue what you mean."

"I'll bet. You look new here."

While they were talking, the giant man backed slowly away, before making an about face and running.

Raincoat didn't pursue. "Ran away, huh? Well, whatever."

She shouldered her shovel, sighing.

The giant man's left arm was still wriggling.

Before Haruhiro fell asleep, there had been a variety of different monsters swarming all over. How about now?

No, they were gone. It was awfully quiet.

There was a something small moving in one of those pink thickets of coral, or plant, or whatever they were made of, and it was casting a white shadow. He didn't sense anything else. There was no wind, either.

That, and, he suddenly realized, the air wasn't sweet.

Raincoat started to stride off.

"...U-Um!" Haruhiro called out without meaning to.

Raincoat kept walking for a few steps. Just as he was thinking, *Ignoring me, huh?* she suddenly stopped, and turned around like it was a hassle.

"What?"

"Uh... I'm not sure what, but, um... where am I?"

"Parano."

"Is that...the name of this place?"

"I don't know. But they call this place Parano."

"Is it one of those things? Like Grimgar, or the Dusk Realm, or Darunggar? Another world?"

"I don't really know why, but Parano's the otherworld, apparently."

"The otherworld..."

The first thing that came to mind when he heard that word was the afterlife.

What did that mean again?

Oh, right.

The world of the dead.

"...Huh? Did I die, maybe...?"

"Maybe." Raincoat let out a nasal laugh. "If so, then maybe everyone here is long dead. The afterlife, huh? It could be."

"...Is it just me?" he ventured. "How about my comrades? Oh, right. Um, there were others with me... Kuzaku, Shihoru, Merry, and Setora. Four of them, I guess. Oh, there should have been a nyaa, too. Do you know anything about them?"

"They might have been here. Might not have. A star fell, and there was a huge commotion. They might have gotten gobbled up by dream monsters. They might've run away. Who knows."

"I'm asking a serious question here..."

"Yeah, and? I have to give a serious answer? Why? Give me a reason."

"The reason is... Okay, there may not be a reason, but..." Haruhiro hung his head.

The giant man's left arm still hadn't stopped moving. Was it still alive? Sickening. It was that thing's arm. It had the same face as him, too.

Haruhiro's dagger was lying on the sandy ground. He picked it up, testing his grip. It was the dagger from the dwarf hole.

This place, it wasn't the afterworld, after all.

"Nah," he murmured. "I dunno about that..."

"Hey, you," Raincoat said.

"Uh... yes?"

"Here."

Raincoat rummaged through the raincoat that had given her her name—though that wasn't really her name, and Haruhiro was just calling her that in his head.

She pulled out something, lightly tossing it to him. It fell to the ground at Haruhiro's feet. It was a blackish cloth, with a string attached.

"A mask?" Haruhiro asked.

"Yeah. You'd better put that on. If you don't, you'll fall asleep every time the wind blows."

"Fall asleep...when the wind blows?"

"The winds of Parano are sweet. If you inhale a lot of the sweet wind, you'll get sleepy. If you sleep, you'll dream. The dreams you see in Parano become real."

While dubious of what exactly Raincoat was trying to say, Haruhiro sheathed his dagger, and crouched to pick up the mask. There were layers of cloth sewn together, and it was thicker than he'd expected. It must have been handmade.

"That thing from before," he said hesitantly. "It was my dream... you said. A dream monster? Right?"

"Before a star falls, the wind always blows. People like you often appear where stars fall."

"Stars..." Haruhiro tried putting the mask on. As might have been expected from its thickness, it made it a little hard to breathe.

"You'll get used to it in no time," Raincoat said, as if seeing right through him.

Haruhiro bowed his head. "Thanks."

Raincoat waved her hand at him as if his thanks were a nuisance, and then took off walking again.

Haruhiro followed. "Erm..."

"What?" Raincoat responded without turning back.

"You haven't always been here, either...have you?"

"Well, no."

"How long have you been here?"

"Who knows."

"You don't?"

"In Parano, you don't have to sleep. In general, you won't even feel sleepy. Not if you don't inhale the sweet wind."

"You don't need sleep?" Haruhiro asked.

"You'll get hungry, and you'll get thirsty, too, but even if you don't eat or drink, it won't kill you."

"Wait... I'll get hungry, but I don't have to eat? That means..."

"If you don't die, you'll find out soon enough."

"What about mornings, and nights?"

"You could say we have them, you could say we don't. It's hard to get a good grasp of time. We apparently don't age in Parano."

"You don't...age?"

"The sense of time, I guess you could call it? That's already gone for me. I can't say this for certain, but we probably don't age."

I may be dead, after all, Haruhiro started to think. *For now, I can definitely say this isn't Grimgar. Even if it's another world, an alternate world, it's way too different. It's completely "other" to everything. Is that why it's the otherworld?*

Raincoat shouldered her shovel, her legs moving with smooth steps.

It was an old shovel. Its cutting edge was incredible, but it wasn't just the blade that was metal, the handle was, too, and they were all rusty. It was blackened all over, and there wasn't a smooth section on the whole thing.

Looking closely, there were cracks here and there all over the shovel, not just on the handle, or just on the blade. From deep inside those cracks there was something red and glossy peeking through, something with a texture unlike metal, like the meat of some animal perhaps. What was that?

More importantly, was it okay to keep following Raincoat?

Raincoat seemed to know Parano, and how to survive here. She was brusque, but had likely saved Haruhiro, and had given him a mask to protect him from the sweet wind. If he stayed with Raincoat, he was safe for now.

But that's just me. His comrades flashed through his mind. Shouldn't he go back and look for them?

Haruhiro turned back as he walked. He let out a strange cry. "Wuh!"

The arm. The giant man's arm, it was there.

Now that he thought about it, the arm had been alive even after the giant man had fled. There was a trail of blood on the path this severed arm, as well as Haruhiro and Raincoat, had taken. It was moving forward by moving its wrist and fingers. Was it chasing them?

"Wh-what..."

...should we do? About this?!

Ignoring the perplexed Haruhiro, Raincoat turned back, and stomped on the giant man's arm. The left arm flailed around like a fish on a hook. "Well, you're full of life. Maybe I can steal the id from this on its own."

"Steal its...id?"

"Let's give it a shot."

Raincoat turned the blade of her shovel downward, grasping the handle with her right hand. She lifted up, then brought the blade down on the giant man's left hand.

Chop! Chop! Chop! She repeated that action several times.

It was just a left arm severed below the elbow, but there was something about this that was hard to watch. Was it because the owner had shared a face with him? Or did that have nothing to do with it? Maybe it did, just a little.

The giant man's left arm eventually stopped writhing. With its flesh and bones all torn up, there was probably no way it could move.

"Hmm..." Raincoat said. "Maybe it went up a bit. My id. Hard to say."

"Um, Raincoat-san?"

"'Raincoat'?"

"...Uh, sorry. I don't know your name... Mine's Haruhiro."

"I'm Alice C," said Alice, using a masculine pronoun to refer to herself.

"C?" Haruhiro repeated.

"It's what they call me here. Alice is fine."

"Alice..." Haruhiro cocked his head to the side.

There was something about that name. It didn't feel right.

The pronoun Alice was using, it was masculine. Could it be that Haruhiro had been making a mistake?

Haruhiro scrutinized Alice's face. It might have been rude, but he couldn't help himself. Well, with the hood over Alice's head, and the mask covering the lower half of her face, Haruhiro could only tell the shape of her eyes, but it was hard to imagine she was male. Her shoulders were thin, and she was probably ten centimeters shorter than him. Also, her head was small. She was petite, overall.

"Uh... sorry," Haruhiro said. "This whole time...I was assuming you were a woman..."

"Oh. I don't care about that stuff."

"No, but... Well, if you say so..."

"Male, female, does it make a difference?"

"Well, I guess...you have a point...?"

"Haruhiro," Alice said.

"...Huh?"

"Welcome to Parano." Alice's eyes narrowed. It was probably a smile.

Haruhiro couldn't help but doubt.

Maybe this is a dream, after all...?

14 | A Vague You and Me

LEAVING THE AREA where thickets of pink coral-like plants grew on white sandy ground, they came out into the foothills of Mt. Glass.

Mt. Glass, as per its name, was made up of hard, translucent rocks that were piled up to form a mountain. According to Alice, the glass was hard but brittle, and if you stepped on the wrong spot, it easily gave way. If it collapsed, they wouldn't get off lightly. They could expect to end up heavily injured at least, or dead at worst.

They scraped the outside of the foothills of Mt. Glass, and it felt like they were walking over white sand for a long while. But that wasn't certain. The flow of time was awfully vague.

Alice's footsteps were dotted across the sand. Haruhiro tried not to step on them. If he did, his footsteps would combine with Alice's, leaving only one set of footsteps behind. When he turned back, two sets of footprints went on for as far as he could see. Not one set, two.

He heard beast-like cries occasionally, and when he looked up at the polka dot sky, there were monsters with shapes which he couldn't imagine were birds flying through it.

How long had it been there? There was a purple crescent floating in the sky, looking awfully big. It felt like if he reached out, he could touch it. He stared at it vacantly.

"Don't look," Alice told him. "If you look directly at Parano's moon, you'll be cursed."

"So it's a moon, huh? That thing."

"What'd you think it was? It doesn't look like anything else."

"I thought it was alive, maybe. One of those...dream monsters, was it?"

"Dream monsters aren't alive. That's why they have no ego."

Honestly, he couldn't understand half of what Alice said. If he asked questions, sometimes he got answers and sometimes he got ignored.

Sometimes...he didn't know anymore. Did Alice really exist? Or was he actually alone, just hallucinating that he was with someone?

No, that wasn't it. There was proof. The footsteps. There were two sets, like there should be. Besides, if he looked in front of him, Alice was there.

But maybe he couldn't trust his senses, or his memory.

Looking like a crown, Mt. Glass was all glass, as far as the eye could see. The foothills were gentle, and the incline eventually became steep. It was beautiful, but nothing special once you got used to seeing it. It was a mountain of glass.

At the border between Mt. Glass and the sandy ground, the white sand was intermingled with small glass rocks. The glass stones weren't as fine as the sand, and they felt totally different underfoot.

When had it happened? He no longer saw any of the pink-colored, coral-like plants. There was a milky and white smoke over the sand. Less of a mist, and more of a cloud.

Was he really walking? Could it be he was actually lying down somewhere, with his eyes closed? When he opened his eyes, would he be in a different place? In front of that door in the Leslie Camp, for instance?

Or perhaps he was nowhere at all. If that was case, then where was the "he" who was thinking he was nowhere at all?

It was all silly. The fact that he could feel things, and think things, was proof of his existence. This was no dream. It was going on way too long to be a dream. It'd be weird if he didn't wake up soon.

Where were Kuzaku... Shihoru... Merry... Setora? Were they safe?

Why didn't he go looking for his comrades?

It was all weird. Maybe this was a dream, after all. Was the lack of logical flow and consistency in his thoughts and actions because it was a dream? If this was a dream, none of it was strange. Anything was possible.

If he were to assume he was dreaming, then when had the dream started?

Hey, Manato, Haruhiro thought. *Was it a dream that you died, too, maybe?*

If it was, this was an awfully long dream. But no matter how long, complicated, and intricate a dream was, the moment he opened his eyes, he'd rapidly forget it. In no time, he'd hardly remember a thing. Maybe it was that sort of dream. Maybe it was that sort of dream... Maybe...

Now that you mention it, I think it is like that, maybe. This dream would become an empty shell like that, and then vanish.

"I'm hungry..." Haruhiro muttered. "My throat's dry, too..."

Either Alice didn't hear, or wasn't listening. It was like Alice C was here, but not here, and continued walking without turning back.

On several occasions, he considered stopping. *I should sit down and rest,* he thought. If Alice got out of sight while he was resting, so be it. There was no Alice anyway. He was alone.

Why couldn't he commit to that? Was he scared? Lonely? What did it matter anymore? He didn't even know if he was alive or not.

"Um, where are you going?" Haruhiro asked. "Hey! Hey, I said! I'm asking you a question here, you know? Why aren't you answering? Don't ignore me. Screw you. What the hell? Put yourself in my shoes here. For a start, why... Why is this happening? Did I have this coming to me...maybe? Not really. It's always like this. Every. Single. Time..."

Haruhiro breathed in deeply.

"Maybe I just think that, though. I feel like the same sort of thing's happened several times now. Am I wrong? Can't trust my memory, after all. Besides... Yeah. I don't remember what happened before I came to Grimgar, either. It's weird. I'm not a two- or three-year-old. If this had all happened before I was old enough to really think, I'd understand. It's not, though. It's weird, right? It's weird. A lot of stuff's happened, but it's all weird. I can't imagine this is reality."

Haruhiro sorted through the thoughts in his head.

"Which means...it's a place that isn't real, basically. It's a dream. A dream. All of it. Manato. Moguzo. Ranta. Shihoru. Yume. Merry. Kuzaku. Setora. All of them, they don't exist. They aren't real. Me...in my head...in my dream, or whatever it is, I created them. They're figments of my imagination. Everything that's happened is. Grimgar, the Dusk Realm, Darunggar, and this world, Parano, too. Man, I'm amazing. The power of my imagination, I mean. It's not half bad, huh? It's pretty crazy... Huh? Then what about me, myself? This me that thinks I'm me... Is that an imagination, too? Is there someone out there somewhere...different from me, dissimilar, maybe not even human, a creature or something...dreaming about me?"

He hesitated.

"No, that's not it. It can't be. But how can I prove it? It's impossible, right? Well, damn... When am I going to wake from this dream? Is it one of those things? Do I have to die? If I die, I think maybe I'll wake up. That could be how it's set up. Manato and Moguzo...and Choco, the ones who died, maybe that's what's happened to all of them. They wake from the dream when they die...and return to their original worlds. But...if so, that's weird, too. I mean, this is my... no, not my, someone else's dream."

Haruhiro was beginning to feel lost.

"If it were a bunch of people's dreams mashed together, that'd be weird. There's nothing. It's all meaningless. Because it's all just a dream... even if I die, it may all be the same. This dream will probably go on forever. Until the dreamer wakes...and when they wake, they'll forget. It'll all return to nothing. To zero... Ahh, I'm hungry. My throat's dry, too. So dry it hurts... This is suffering."

He tore off his mask and threw it away. He wanted to strip off his cloak and his clothes, too, cast everything off.

The wind was blowing. Sweet. The air was sweet. He sucked in all he could, and choked on it. It reminded him of something.

Oh. Vanilla. It was like the scent of vanilla.

He inhaled. Exhaled. Inhaled. Inhaled, inhaled, inhaled as deeply as he could.

It was incredibly sweet. He could feel the sweetness up to his eyeballs. The more he inhaled, the more he suffered. Still, he didn't stop.

"Hey!" Suddenly, he was grabbed by the collar and shaken.

It was Alice. Right in front of his eyes. Alice.

To hell with Alice C.

"Don't breathe the wind! Do you want to fall asleep and give birth to another dream monster?!"

"I don't care."

"Your ego's gotten pretty weak," Alice snapped. "At this rate, you'll go mad. You won't get off with just falling asleep and creating a dream monster. Do you want to fall to darkness, and become a trickster?"

"I have. No clue. What you're talking about."

"One of my friends fell to darkness. Once that happens, there's no coming back. I can't turn you back, at least. Nui is..."

"...Nui?"

"Just listen!"

Alice pushed Haruhiro down. When he landed on his backside, it cleared the haze from his mind, and the sweetness clinging to the inside of his lungs made him feel sick.

Alice picked up the mask, throwing it at Haruhiro's face. "Put it on. I didn't save you so you could fall to darkness."

Haruhiro tried to put the mask on. His fingers trembled, and it wasn't working.

While he was fumbling around, Alice stabbed the shovel into the ground, knelt down, and snatched the mask from Haruhiro's hands. "Listen, Haruhiro. You know how people sometimes tell you to keep a hold of yourself? In Parano, that's really important."

Alice put the mask on for him. Haruhiro didn't move a muscle. Or rather, he was tense, and he couldn't move.

"No matter what anyone may say or think about me, I know who I am, and no matter what happens, I will not be anything that isn't me. That's ego. It can't be expressed in numbers, but in Parano, you can sense whether someone's ego is weak or strong. You can't see it. It's like a smell, or a taste. If you want to remain yourself, you have to be yourself. If you don't, you'll become something other than yourself. I don't mean that metaphorically. You will actually turn into something else. Into what's called a trickster."

"That what I...started to turn into?"

Alice stood up, pulling the shovel out of the ground. "If I'd left you alone, I think you would have, yeah."

Haruhiro looked around the area. To his right, Mt. Glass rose up to the sky, the glass foothills and white sand mixed together, and at the end of it all was smoke.

Like always, the more he looked at it, the more his sense of reality seemed to weaken. It was a rather vague scene.

"Where are you heading... if you don't mind me asking?" he hesitated.

"To where I live."

"A house?"

"You'll understand if you come. If you can get there intact, that is," Alice said brusquely, then shouldered the shovel and started walking.

"I have to be myself..." Haruhiro murmured to himself as he followed Alice.

I... Myself... Does that mean acting in a way that's like me? What does that mean?

What am I?

If I had a mirror, I could look at my face in it. That's me. But sadly, I don't have a mirror. Well, it's not like I'd want to see my own face. I'm not in the habit of looking closely at it, anyway. So...

If you were to ask if I remember in detail what I look like, it's doubtful. Even if the face in the mirror changed slightly, I might not notice.

Still, the one stepping on the white sand mixed with small bits of glass, footsteps crunching, that's unquestionably me, myself. I feel the weight of my body. The hunger, and the thirst, too. Those feelings undoubtedly belong to me.

That means I'm here. If it weren't me here, I wouldn't feel anything, after all.

Well, hey, wasn't that simple?

The one looking at, listening to, smelling, feeling, thinking, pondering about me and things that are not me, that's me. Even if I were to turn into something else, something not quite human maybe, so long as I could look, listen, smell, feel, think, that's still me.

Alice was walking with the shovel shouldered. A gap had opened between them. Alice was about ten meters ahead.

While walking, Haruhiro looked down to his right palm. "...Huh?"

Were my hands always like this? Furry, oversized, with long, sharp claws?

No.

"That's not my hand."

Before he could think, *What do I do?* his left hand was already drawing the flame dagger from the dwarf hole.

Right, I have to cut it off. I mean, this right hand isn't mine. I have to cut it off with this flame dagger. The hand holding the dagger, it's weird, it's all furry, isn't it?

"Dammit! Oboaba! Bugegagobuda! Udebagazo! Nndebanba! Doga!"

Someone's shouting something. Not me. That's not my voice, after all. It shouldn't be. The words, they fiil rong gigazuzu. Badagu dota obada godoga ganbaze gotoga? Onto furebure tobagonda guzoda bugo, oada?

"Haruhiro!" Alice shouted.

"Nnaka?!"

"Look! Look at me!"

"Lu... uk..."

Luuk.

Look.

He looked.

Alice was there.

The one holding his hands, it was Alice.

The color of Alice's eyes, it was pale. He'd thought they seemed bright, but they went past light brown, to almost being the color of blood running through someone's arteries. The hood was pulled back, then finally pulled off, showing Alice's hair.

The color of Alice's hair wasn't so much bright, as pale. Looking closely, the eyebrows and eyelashes were the same color. Alice's skin, too... the word "white" didn't quite adequately describe it. It seemed translucent, like you could see through to the other side of it.

"Get a hold of yourself," Alice said.

Alice was speaking to him.

Haruhiro nodded, looking at his own hands.

Not furry, not big, not with long claws. His own hands.

"It felt...like I wasn't me..."

"The work of a dazzler, huh?"

Alice pushed Haruhiro away, pulling the nearby shovel from

the ground, and swiveling around quickly. There was apparently something behind Haruhiro and to the left.

Alice jumped, swinging the shovel.

The shovel's blade slammed down into the sandy earth.

Just before it did, he felt like he saw a large fish-like thing poking its head out, or maybe he didn't. Either way, by the time Alice buried their shovel in the sand, that thing wasn't there anymore. Had it dived into the sand, just in time?

"You're not getting away!" Alice gripped the shovel with both hands.

What? Huh? What the? It was a shovel...wasn't it? It seemed, at the very least, it wasn't just your ordinary rusty shovel.

The dark, rust-like stuff was its skin, and it had started peeling on its own. The insides were peeking out through cracks in that skin. This might not be the right way to describe it, but it was like a stick made of meat. The skin hadn't fallen off completely, with the ends of it still attached to the meat stick, split into tens of thin belts... no, more than that...and they were all wriggling.

They were as thick as human fingers, and might have looked a bit like black, or dark brown, snakes.

That part was wrapped around Alice. There were some wrapping around the shovel itself, while Alice dove deeper and deeper into the sand.

Was that shovel alive? It wasn't even a shovel to begin with, for sure. No way could there be a shovel like that. If it wasn't a shovel, what was it? No other appropriate name came to mind, so it would have to be called a shovel for now.

When Alice suddenly pulled up the shovel, it had hooked it.

Had their target been caught by the black snakey things, which had pulled it from the sand, forcing it out?

It had hands and feet, more or less being humanoid, and sort of resembled a sahuagin. Those eyes and that mouth were especially fish-like. But its light peach skin was strangely smooth. It had been in the sand all this time, but for some reason it wasn't covered in sand.

"The work of a dazzler," Alice had said.

A dazzler. Was that what this thing was called?

"Looks kind of like an axolotl, huh," Alice muttered, and then the black snakes holding the dazzler shrunk away.

The freed dazzler immediately jumped up.

It turned its back on Alice, likely trying to get away.

But unfortunately—no, not unfortunately at all—Alice cut off any hope of that. By cutting the dazzler.

Alice stepped forward, thrusting out with the shovel. The shovel's blade pierced the dazzler through its back.

Alice pulled the shovel upward in that state. The shovel easily sliced the dazzler from its breast to the top of its head.

There was no splatter of blood. What seeped out of the dazzler's wound instead was a thick mucus that was like old oil.

The dazzler fell forward.

"Finally got it."

Chop, chop, chop. Alice used the shovel, to stab, slice, cut up, and dismember the dazzler, then snorted. Alice was probably happy about having killed the dazzler, but also looked to be enjoying this brutal work.

"That one wasn't a dream monster. It was a half-monster. When humans are taken in by dream monsters, they turn into half-monsters like this dazzler."

"Taken...in..."

"Most dream monsters just attack and eat people, though. Still, there are some weird ones. I wonder about that dream monster you made. By the way, unlike dream monsters that have nothing but id, half-monsters have ego, too. Not much, though. If you kill them, you can take it all. Half-monsters are rare, so they're valuable."

Alice's shoulders heaved with laughter.

Suddenly, a thought occurred to Haruhiro. Alice looked human, but was Alice really?

Just because Alice looked human didn't mean that was true. He didn't know what these dream monsters and half-monsters were, but maybe they were something different like that.

Haruhiro backed away. It was dangerous to trust Alice. But Alice had saved him. Alice was going out of their way to bring Haruhiro back to where Alice lived. What for? Out of simple kindness? Did Alice have some reason, some ulterior motive?

It might be a trap.

Alice's hands stopped. For a moment, he worried Alice was about to spring at him.

Those fears were unfounded. Though it was a little late, Alice seemed to realize the hood had come off.

Alice put it back on, and resumed work.

Grimgar of Fantasy and Ash

15 | With Faces Uncovered

AFTER A FEW HOURS, half a day, or longer than that—basically, a really long time—he noticed something he hadn't paid attention to before, even though they had been walking on the border between Mt. Glass and the sandy ground the whole time.

The sand was flowing, albeit slowly.

What was more, it wasn't in any one fixed direction. In one place, the sand would move towards the foothills. In another, a little further along, it would be moving towards Haruhiro and Alice. There were even times when the sand would flow in the same direction they were moving, making it easier to move, like a wind at their backs.

If he looked real closely, the foothills which were buried in shards of glass weren't unmoving, either. If he listened, there was a tiny sound.

Clink, clink, clink, clink...

It wasn't enough to be visible to the eye, but there was a subtle movement going on.

"The geography of Parano is mutable," Alice said. "Nothing is unchanging. Nothing, okay?"

That's what Alice C said, he thought.

But when had he heard it? What had made Alice tell him that? He thought about it, but it was unclear.

Eventually, from beyond the sandy ground with its milky white smoke, some sort of shadow began to show itself. Was it a forest? The lines were too straight for that. Buildings then, maybe? It wasn't just one. There were multiple buildings packed tightly together. Was it a town?

"Is that where you...?" he began, to which Alice simply replied, "Yeah."

"How far, from here to there?"

"Depends."

"Huh...?"

"We all feel things differently."

In Parano, time and space existed, but they might as well not have.

Long ago, Alice told him on the way to town, so long ago that it wasn't clear exactly when, but it was probably "way back," Alice had tried to make a clock.

In Parano's sky, there was a moon and stars. Yet there was no sun. That meant a sundial was out of the question, so Alice had decided on a water clock.

Alice had wanted something that, even if it didn't tell the

precise time, kept time using roughly fixed intervals. The first one was simple: a small hole in the bottom of a container, markings carved into the inside. When the container was filled with water, the water slowly drained out the bottom. If the rate of outflow was fixed, it should have been possible to use it as a measure of time.

However, when Alice had actually tried to do it, various problems had arisen.

For instance, the container. Even if it was a large container, if there was a slope between the mouth and the bottom of it, it didn't work well. As the volume of water in the container decreased, the force with which it came out the hole fell, too.

Even once those problems were worked around, others arose. Through the process of trial and error, the water clock had ended up becoming as large as a tower, using a non-trivial amount of water. Eventually Alice had gotten fed up with it, smashing the water clock it had taken so much work to build into little pieces.

While listening to the story, Haruhiro started to doubt it. Had it really happened? Was it just a made-up story?

For one thing, it wasn't like Alice to tell long-winded stories. Was Alice the one talking? Was it something else?

No, Alice was talkative. He was starting to get that feeling. It wasn't like he knew Alice all that well to begin with. It'd be fair to say he knew practically nothing. Wasn't it messed up for him to say what was or wasn't like Alice?

Seriously, it's messed up.

Everything here is.

Including me.

As they got closer to the town, the haze cleared. They weren't on sandy ground anymore. The ground was dirt. When had that happened? He hadn't noticed the transition at all.

There were grass and trees growing. The bark was brown, and the leaves were green. He thought these were normal plants, but when he stepped on them, they blew to pieces, leaving no trace in no time. They were like hallucinations. That, or illusions.

The buildings were fairly tall. Like giant stone pillars. There were rectangular holes lined up systematically across their surface. They had windows, but the windows lacked glass panes, or even wooden shutters, so they looked like some sort of nests, too.

The buildings had no doubt all stood upright at one point. But now, some had collapsed, while others were leaning.

Because he had been vacantly staring up at the buildings, Alice's figure seemed far away. He quickened his pace to catch up.

"Um, what is this place?"

"Ruins No. 6," she said. "Before it came to be called that, it was a town called Asoka, I hear."

"Asoka..."

"That's just a thing I heard, though."

"Are there...people here? Erm... Other than you, I mean."

"No one sane," Alice said with a little laugh.

"That includes you, I suppose? Princess." It was a husky, male voice. Not Alice's.

Looking up, someone was leaning out of a window on what was probably the third floor of a building on their left. He wore a green cloak, along with boots. From the look of him, he was a human man. He had longish, wavy black hair, and a short beard.

"...Ahiru." Alice glared at the man, lowering the shovel from their shoulder. It looked ready to peel again, like when Alice had killed the dazzler.

The man cocked his head to the side, then smirked. "Don't make such a scary face, princess."

"Then don't call me that."

"But you *are* a princess, aren't you?"

"You want to die, Ahiru?"

"I don't, which is why I won't fight you straight-up."

"Don't hang around me."

"Then go back to the king," Ahiru said. "You do that, and I'll never show up in front of you again. I swear."

"There's no way I'll go back."

"The king is mad. If you won't go back, there'll be trouble."

"Not for me, there won't."

"For me, there will."

"Yonaki Uguisu, huh?"

The moment Alice said those words, Ahiru's right leg started to tremble. His knee was going up and down, as if keeping a rhythm. Though he wore a slight smile, he was shaken up inside, or infuriated maybe.

Alice stabbed the shovel into the ground twice, then three times. "How brave of you, Ahiru."

The wind blew. Even with a mask on, it tasted a little sweet.

Ahiru pressed his sleeve to his mouth. "That guy," he said,

looking at Haruhiro. "He's new, isn't he? What are you planning to do, princess? Boil him and eat him? Or bake him and eat him?"

"I'm not a dream monster. I don't eat humans."

"If you eat humans, you can steal their ego and build it up fast. You wanna get stronger, don't you, princess? If you do, eat that guy."

"Shut up, Ahiru. I'll seriously kill you."

"I'll be back, princess." Leaving them with those words, Ahiru vanished inside the window.

There were no entrances or exits to the building other than windows. Alice tried heading towards the building where Ahiru presumably was, but soon came to a stop, head cocked to the side.

Haruhiro sensed something was off, too. It was not so much a sound, as a vibration. The ground was shaking.

Haruhiro turned back. There was a building almost directly opposite from the one Ahiru was in. It was heavily damaged, with cracks throughout it like a spider's web, and it looked like it might be leaning their way a bit, too.

Not long after there was the snapping sound of something hard breaking, a scraping sound, and a terrifying low rumbling from the earth shaking. Could it be—

It's not the ground?

The shaking, was it from that building?

"Run!" Alice took off running before the word was finished.

Haruhiro ran, too.

The building quickly came down behind them. He didn't turn back to check. The sound, the impact, and the cloud of dust were so incredible, there was no need to check and see. He didn't have time, either.

It wasn't just that building. This place, Ruins No. 6, had tens of buildings, possibly more. There was nothing but buildings up ahead, too. Alice and Haruhiro were moving down a road between the buildings. It might not have been all of them, but they were collapsing here and there.

"Damn you, Ahiru!" Alice shouted.

Alice didn't go straight, but turned right and left. It was less that they had some plan in mind, and more they were changing direction each time they spotted a dangerous building.

"Alice...!" Haruhiro shouted.

"You're so annoying! Shut up and follow me!"

Of course, he had no choice but to do that. Haruhiro didn't know this place. He could get out of Ruins No. 6 if he turned back the way they'd come, but that road was no doubt blocked by the rubble of the first building that fell. He had no idea which way was the right way to go.

The moment they turned right, the building in front of them started coming down like it had been liquefied. When they turned left and continued that direction for a little while, two buildings on either side fell over, hitting each other.

As they raced desperately under the falling fragments, he felt like this was all driving him crazy, and it was hard to maintain his sanity.

Somehow he got the feeling that this wasn't a good mental state to be in.

He was drenched with sweat, but his whole body felt cold, and his stomach felt like it was trying to escape out his mouth. For now, he wanted to be out of here, to escape this situation. How long was this going to last for?

Give me a break, he pleaded.

He wanted this to be over soon. No matter how he wished for that, reality wouldn't cater to his needs. When things didn't end, they didn't end.

But what about here, in Parano?

If he really wanted to end it, there was a way.

A way to end it all right now.

An emergency exit, you could say.

If he couldn't do anything else, he could just go out it.

Haruhiro could see that emergency exit. No, he couldn't see it. He just sensed it. It was always behind him, wide open.

To be more precise, it might be more accurate to say it was right in the back of his head. So, even if he turned around, it was still behind him. He couldn't see it, but it was there.

The emergency exit beckoned Haruhiro.

Come, it said. Come to me.

There's no need to hold back. It's not good for you.

Leave the rest to me...

Maybe I should? he wondered. All he had to do was hand himself over to it. If he did, he'd be set free from all the fear, and all the hassle.

No.

He knew he couldn't.

Emergency exits don't speak. Besides, what does that mean, an emergency exit?

Leaving through a door in the back of his head? It was impossible. It couldn't be done. But in Parano, those impossible things happened. Besides, this was, yeah, it was an emergency evacuation. What choice did he have?

Haruhiro came to a stop. He was tired, after all. He didn't want to move anymore.

I think I did a good job.

Did you now?

Yeah, I did well.

Maybe you did.

Isn't it about time?

"Ahh..."

Spreading his legs, he stretched as wide as he could. He ended up looking upwards.

There was a massive piece of debris, ten times the size of a person, coming down.

"Oh, wow!" He could feel a laugh coming.

It was coming right at him. How could he not laugh? He wondered, should he close his eyes, or should he not? It'd be a shame to miss it, so why not watch until the end?

He reached out, and it was almost there. He could almost touch the debris.

"Hahh...!" Alice rushed back, and provided unwanted assistance. The shovel pointed in his direction peeled, and the black belts of skin pierced the debris, pulverizing it into dust.

The debris rained down like hail. Some of it was fist-sized, so of course he wasn't unharmed.

"Ow! Ow, ow, ow, ow..."

He was hit on the left shoulder, the right arm, and the head by large pieces of debris. Was that why he fell over?

He was on his belly, groaning, when he was forcibly dragged to his feet.

"What the hell are you doing?! Come on!"

Alice.

It was Alice again.

"Why can't you leave me alone?!" Haruhiro wailed.

Even as he whined and complained, he moved his legs which it felt like he could sprain at any moment, and he was running for some reason.

Wasn't it pointless to run? There were buildings collapsing in every direction. The clouds of dust made visibility poor. He hurt all over, too.

It was obvious without even thinking. They were done for. There was no way out of this. So, yeah. He was evacuating. There was an end to everything. The end would come someday. Why couldn't it be now?

I've had enough, he thought.

He had his regrets. But no lingering attachment.

"Damn that Ahiru! He's the worst! Haruhiro, come on...!"

His arm was grabbed, and he was pulled along. There was no point in resisting, so he let it happen to him.

Nothing had any meaning.

What was going on?

He wasn't interested, but Alice hugged him close, that shovel stripped itself again, and a number of those black belts of skin, a very large number, came together to form an umbrella. It reached the ground in an instant, neatly enveloping Alice and Haruhiro.

What was going on outside the umbrella? He could more or less imagine. Probably the buildings all collapsed, and the rubble formed a muddy vortex.

Protected by the umbrella, they were standing in the middle of it.

Dark. It was almost completely dark. But he could see a little.

The shovel. The naked shovel glowed faintly. Because of that, it was slightly bright.

Alice was bent over, holding onto the naked shovel firmly, and hugging Haruhiro. It was almost like they were huddled together, in a tiny tent made for one person.

Was that it? Outside, there was a storm. Not your average violent rainstorm. Well, that was a given, since there wasn't any wind or rain.

There was grinding and crunching and scratching and banging. The noise was intense. The shovel had to be under a massive amount of pressure from outside. It was bizarre that it didn't seem to budge one bit under it, but it still felt threatening.

This, when Haruhiro had just been thinking he was fine with it ending here.

"Will it hold?" he asked.

"It's fine. Who do you think I am?"

Was Alice putting up a strong front? It didn't look like it.

"I don't know," were the words that slipped from Haruhiro's mouth. "Honestly, I have no clue who or what you are."

"I'll bet," Alice said with a laugh. "I mean, you don't even know who you are yourself."

"That's not true."

"It is, though. Haruhiro. That ass Ahiru was asking why I don't eat you, but listen. I don't eat people. I mean, people eating people? That's just gross. But if I were to eat someone, it wouldn't be you. Even if I ate you, I'd gain nothing. Your ego is weak. In order to make my magic stronger, I need a strong id, or a strong ego."

"...Magic? You're...a mage?"

"In Parano, anyone can use magic. A magic that is theirs alone. My magic...is this." Alice gripped the naked shovel tight. "It's Philia."

He had no idea what that meant. The shovel was magic, or something? Anyway, he'd been calling it the shovel for sake of convenience, but it was obviously not a shovel.

What the hell is that thing? Haruhiro thought to himself. I dunno if it's called Philia, or what. When it's naked like that, it's damn creepy. My ego's weak? Okay, yeah, if you say that to me, I feel like maybe it is. But so what? Is that wrong?

It's all a dream. I'm having a bad dream. I felt that way this whole time, and I want it to be true.

But I'm pretty sure this isn't a dream...

This is the worst.

It's cruel.

This situation is beyond cruel.

How exactly is it cruel? I don't know. I don't want to think about it.

I'm trying not to think things like, "I'm the only one who survived."

I was doing my best not to think. It's better not to. I mean, if I think things like that, I'll fall. I'll fall all the way, all the way down. And then, in no time—Look.

Here. This is the bottom.

The bottom of a hole that's deep, so deep that it's a wonder I can still breathe.

The bottom of hell.

"Haruhiro."

"...What?"

"Are you crying?"

"Am not."

"It's okay." Alice lightly tapped Haruhiro on the back, as if soothing a child.

What did Alice take him for? Still, it wasn't unpleasant.

Alice might be right. Even though it was about himself, not anyone else, he didn't know a thing.

"It's okay to cry," Alice said. "I don't mind. But it's not okay to drown in tears. Why are you crying? If you're crying without reason, that's not good. Don't think; look at yourself. Don't avert your eyes. Even if it's not what you want to see, you have to look."

"I..."

"You?"

"I'm..."

He covered his face with both hands.

Ahh, this...

This was his face. A face covered with both hands.

He couldn't see his face.

"There is none," he mumbled. "No me. It doesn't exist. I'm not...anywhere. There's nothing... Nothing to me..."

"You're here, Haruhiro. You're here, next to me."

"But I..."

"It's okay to take it a little at a time. What is precious to you?"

"Precious..."

Kuzaku.

Shihoru. Yume.

Merry.

Setora, too... he was worried about her.

Were Setora and Kiichi one and the same?

Ranta.

Damn it. Stupid Ranta. When you're not around... somehow, it all feels so bland.

"I don't like this," Haruhiro whispered. "Everyone..."

Because everyone needs me, I...

Because everyone is there...

I have everyone...

Everyone...

"I'm scared," he whispered.

Without everyone, I'm...

"I'm so uneasy... I can't help myself..." he whispered. "My comrades, they're gone. I don't know if they're safe. I want to think they are...but I can't. I just can't. It may be no good. This time... this may be it. No way. Am I...all alone now?"

"You have me, don't you?" Alice asked.

"Oh, yeah. You're here. You... I can't tell if you're kind, or cruel."

"The thing about me is, I can be kind at times, and cruel at others."

At some point, things outside settled.

It was tight inside, and hard to breathe, but warm.

Who and what was Alice C?

16 | A Multifaceted Personality

I HAVE ANOTHER NAME, you know. The one my parents gave me. But I've always been called Alice.

I was bullied. Not teased a little. Outright bullied.

As for the reason I got called Alice, it's the fault of the book I was reading. Okay, that's a bit unfair to say it's the book's "fault." Books can do no wrong. But still, I hated being called Alice.

"Alice!"

"I'm not Alice."

"Aaaalice!"

"I'm not Alice."

"Aaaaliiiice!"

"I told you, I'm not Alice!"

"Aliiiice!"

"You don't give up. Whatever. Say what you want."

"Then it's okay, right, Alice?"

"Aaaalice!"

"Aaaaliiiice!"

"Alice!"

"Aliiiice!"

"Alice!"

I remember, just like that, it was like I'd given them permission. Anyone and everyone started calling me Alice, Alice, Alice, Alice, Alice, Alice, Alice, Alice, Alice.

They hid my stuff. Broke it sometimes, too. They scribbled on my things, and threw stuff at me.

Also, and this one I remember vividly, there was this thing they called the Apology Game. They'd surround me in the park, so I couldn't move. Then I'd tell them to get out of the way, clear the road, or whatever. They wouldn't, of course. That would piss me off, so I'd try pushing them aside.

Then they'd make an exaggerated show of falling over, saying it hurt, or they'd broke a bone, or they were bleeding, or some other nonsense.

"Apologize! Apologize!" they'd demand. They wouldn't let me off until I did.

It wasn't like they would let me off when I did it, either. I'd be told to say it with more sincerity, or if I was really sorry I should do this, or that. They demanded a lot from me that way.

They outnumbered me, see.

They'd shout at me, too. I would have no choice but to do as they said.

As for what they made me do, I'll leave that to your imagination.

Well, the things they did, when I remember them, it's worse than just feeling bile rising in my throat; I want to dash my own head open.

The key point is, they didn't hold me down to do things to me. I was forced, that's for sure, but I did it myself. I hate the ones who put me through it, obviously. But I blame myself for meekly obeying, too.

In the end, I have to wonder if maybe it was my own fault for being weak. If I hated it so much, I should have bitten through my own tongue. I should have been able to bite them like I had gone mad, too. I wonder why I didn't.

The name Alice—to me, it's a wound.

Not a scar, a wound. One that's big, always raw, and will never fade.

I hate myself more than I can handle. I hate everything about myself, and more than anything, I can't forgive myself for being like this.

Or so I was feeling back then, anyway.

I was cursing it all.

The whole world, you see.

It all started when I came to Parano, I guess.

That was when I came to realize that even I, who cursed everything, had things I'd loved, things that were important to me.

For instance, I thought I detested this face, this body of mine, but despite that, I was always looking in the mirror. Pretty closely, actually.

The truth is, I'd think, Oh, I don't look too bad from this angle, or, That expression just now, that was pretty nice, as I was looking in the mirror.

If someone said, *What're you staring at that mirror for?* back then, I'd have denied it. *No, I'm not looking!* But thinking back now, I was looking.

My looks are unusual, but not ugly, I mean. Not that it'd be bad if they were. The things commonly seen as ugly, like cleft chins, snub noses, thick lips, a big belly, they can be cute if you look at them right.

I hated myself, but there were parts of me I liked.

Or rather, as I was bullied, I started to think it was my own fault, and I began to hate that about myself. You could say that I was forced into hating and detesting myself.

It wasn't that I hated everything about myself. There were bits that pissed me off, sure, but part I was deeply in love with, too.

Then...I realized. I couldn't take them teasing me, calling me Alice, Alice, Alice. But I didn't hate the name itself.

In fact, I now feel like Alice fits me better than the name my parents gave me.

Am I cruel, or kind? The answer is, I'm both.

The people who did those awful things to me, it's not like they were total scum all the time. They'd feel bad seeing a poor abandoned cat on the brink of death, and help their families and friends when they were in trouble.

There were probably some who, even though they were participating in the Apology Game, were thinking, *Whoa, that's rough. We didn't have to go this far.*

One even had pangs of conscience, and covertly sent me a letter. It was in the mailbox. The sender didn't write their name, but it was neatly written by hand.

When the bullying was at its worst, I did some pretty nasty stuff myself. Like pulling the wings and legs off bugs. Anytime I would watch them writhe in that state, it made me feel better. When I was done, I'd say, *I think it's about time I put you out of your misery,* and then kill them.

I thought about doing the same to larger animals. I never did, though. Not because I felt bad for them. It just felt like it would be a lot of hassle, so I didn't. If it had been easy, I think I would have. It might've escalated from there, with me ending up a proper serial killer one day.

Naturally, if I hadn't been bullied for so long, I don't think it'd have ever occurred to me to do things like that. Even so, I can't say I'm not a cruel person.

To give an example, imagine a game where several people, including yourself, are locked in a closed room, and only one can emerge alive.

What would you do in that situation?

Would you kill the others, and survive yourself?

Or would you let yourself be killed, because murder is wrong?

Would you commit suicide?

There's some merit in the argument that the situation proposed is too extreme, and it's inappropriate to try and glean anything about the nature of you, as a person, from it.

But anything can happen. It's not a completely impossible

situation. You're in Parano, too, so you understand, right?

I don't know how or where you came to Parano from, but I was at a school by the seaside. There was a cave in a cliff along the shore, and people were talking about exploring it.

Around that time, I was using the strategies I'd learned for dealing with bullying, and I was getting by reasonably well thanks to a number of coincidences. It felt like if I screwed up, I'd be right back where I was before, though.

I had a number of friends, and one of them invited me to go with them, so I had no real reason to refuse.

Into the pitch-black cave we went, progressing deeper and deeper.

At some point along the way, it was like there was gas. Our vision got worse, and I remember feeling like it was bad news. But all I can say is, the next thing I knew, I was here.

We had carelessly wandered into Parano.

It was beyond unexpected. That something so ridiculous could happen, I mean.

If a person kills other people because some situation has left them no other choice, that's a person who is capable of killing. If that opportunity had never come along, they might have gone their whole lives without killing anyone, though.

Me, I can kill.

If the need arises, I'll kill anyone, and anything, with my own hands. No regrets. I mean, if I had to do it, I had to do it.

But I do at least have emotions.

Back then, a star fell. Based on my experience, I figured

someone had come to Parano, so I went to check. That's how I found you. I couldn't leave you alone, so I saved you.

You're not my friend, or anything else to me. You, personally, are nothing special. But there's no one sane in Parano, so I get nostalgic sometimes.

When I see a decent person like you, doing nothing but care for others while being empty yourself, gradually becoming only the you who is reflected in the eyes of others, like some sort of flimsy mirror person, it makes me want to talk so badly.

Well, that's all, though, really.

I've already accomplished my objective, so I'm pretty satisfied.

I might abandon you like you're nothing. But, like I said, I can be kind sometimes. When I'm nice to others like this, it feels good. But I may get sick of it eventually.

That, or change my mind, and decide I want to eat you. I don't have any plans for it yet, but I might take advantage of you somehow. Or trick you. When the time comes, I'll say so.

If you tell the person you're about to trick that you're going to trick them, they won't fall for it, you say?

You idiot. I've done it before.

By the way, what do you want to do?

What do you want me to do for you?

Grimgar of Fantasy and Ash

17 |

Things That Change, Things That Don't

How long had they been buried alive? It was pointless to think about it. Time held no meaning in Parano. Even if he'd had a mechanical watch, it would probably have stopped, started, turned clockwise, turned counterclockwise, and been utterly useless.

Alice C had used the magic shovel to dig a passage to the surface, making it easy to escape.

Once they were out, Ruins No. 6 had been reduced to a pile of rubble. Very few buildings remained—six of them to be exact—and they were all half-destroyed, or buried in the rubble.

"Looks like that's the end of my hideout," Alice said. "Damn Ahiru. Next time we meet, he's dead."

"This was all Ahiru's doing?" Haruhiro asked.

"I told you. In Parano, anyone can use magic. Ahiru's magic is the same type as mine."

"Philia? Or whatever it was called?"

"Yeah," Alice's eyes narrowed, and there was a laugh.

Haruhiro still hadn't seen Alice without the mask. What sort of face did that person have?

"Magic in Parano can be widely broken up into three types... no, make that four types. But I've never seen the fourth. There's philia, narci, and doppel. Magic generally falls into one of these three types."

Alice went on to explain what those meant.

Philia was love. Love used curses to imbue a specific object, like a commonly used item, or a weapon used to protect oneself, with power. These were called fetishes.

"The source of philia is the fetish," Alice said, lifting the shovel. "The charmed item makes the holder stronger, giving them magic. If they lose hold of the fetish, the owner weakens, becoming unable to use magic. I've killed dream monsters with this. It seemed weird to go spelunking empty-handed, so we figured we should bring some tools. I was holding it. Not by coincidence. I don't know why, but I wanted to carry it. I said I would, and I was allowed to. Maybe I had a premonition or something. In the end, it saved me."

"So...that shovel became a fetish?" Haruhiro asked slowly.

"Haruhiro, you have a knife or something like it, right?" Alice asked. "Maybe it'll become your fetish. Maybe it won't. By the way, Ahiru's fetish is a belt. The one around his waist."

"How'd he topple that many buildings with a belt?"

"Search me. I'll bet he worked hard at it, prepping every building one by one."

"That seems like it'd take a whole lot of time."

"Whether it did or didn't, it's all the same in this place. You either do something, or you don't. Ahiru did. He's weaker than I am, but he has a goal, and he won't give up. He can't beat me, so he harasses me, and tries to call me to the king's palace."

"The king?" Haruhiro repeated.

He was ignored. Alice didn't answer questions Alice didn't want to answer.

There were hardly any flat spots in the sea of debris, so they climbed up and down, repeatedly jumping over and diverting around obstacles as they gradually made progress.

In the beginning, Alice went ahead, and Haruhiro followed behind in silence. But gradually Alice would stop more and more to sigh and swing the shovel around pointlessly. She seemed sick of this, so the choice of course was apparently not very efficient.

When Haruhiro took the lead instead, having Alice just to decide the general direction, they picked up the pace considerably.

"Could it be that you're used to this?" Alice asked.

"Uh... Well, yeah," Haruhiro said. "Reasonably so."

"Hmm. Were you living like a survivalist, or something?"

"It's a long story."

"You don't get it. You don't need to worry whether the story's long or short."

So, as Haruhiro walked from one piece of rubble that looked like a viable foothold to another, he told Alice all about himself, or rather his group.

He didn't start at the beginning, which was when they woke

up in Grimgar more than a year and a half ago. He didn't go through all the events in order. He'd jump from here to there, moving back and forth. He was, he would have to admit himself, a bad storyteller. Or maybe, because this was Parano, it was just naturally turning out that way.

When they were finally out of Ruins No. 6, there was water spread out over a wide area just past the white sand. There was no current. Was it a lake? In the distance, there was a milky white smoke.

"Where is this?" Haruhiro asked, but Alice shrugged.

"I'd have to guess I probably haven't seen it before. There aren't many places that have existed all along. As far as I know, there are Ruins No. 1 through Ruins No. 7, which are the remains of seven towns and their surroundings, Mt. Glass, the Iron Tower of Heaven, the Valley of Worldly Desire, and the Sanzu River."

"The rest change?"

"If you remember all the landmarks, you'll get by fine."

"Ruins No. 6 doesn't vanish, then," Haruhiro pondered. "That's why you were living there, huh?"

"That bastard Ahiru really got me this time."

"You think he got caught up in it, too?"

"He's stubborn, so I figure he's alive. If he were dead, I couldn't kill him. I need him alive."

Alice walked out onto the surface of the water like it was no big deal. Did they plan to swim?

When Alice's right foot touched the surface, ripples spread out from there. They didn't sink.

Was it not water? It seemed it was a surface that was clear and that reflected light like water. What was more, when stimulated, it produced ripples.

The bottom wasn't visible. It was just clear all the way.

Haruhiro tried walking, too. When the ripples that spread with each step touched, they negated one another. If not interrupted by another ripple, they would spread out forever.

"First, we need to find a place to settle down," Alice said, making many ripples.

"I want to search for my comrades," Haruhiro said.

"I heard that. You want my help, too, I'm sure. Well, honestly, I doubt they're alive, and searching for people here isn't simple."

"You said it's a matter of whether we do a thing or don't, Alice. That being the case, I'll do it."

"'My comrades. Everyone. Everyone. My comrades.' That's all you ever say. If your comrades told you to go die, would you do it?"

"If that were the best option."

"Plenty of guys who'd say that are all talk, but you might actually go and do it."

"I don't say things I don't think."

"If I help you, what's in it for me?" Alice demanded.

"Ahiru has a goal, you said. What about you? You just want to get stronger?"

He got ignored again. Alice probably didn't want to say.

"If you help me, I'll help you in equal measure," Haruhiro said at last.

"You?" Alice laughed out loud.

It didn't even offend him that much.

Alice had said that anyone could use magic in Parano. But Haruhiro had yet to discover his magic. Alice was probably thinking, *What can you even do?*

"You can decide whether I'm of any use later," Haruhiro answered.

"No, Haruhiro, I don't think you're useless. You were a thief, right? It sounds like something out of a game, but you can use those skills here, can't you?"

"A game?"

"They show up in RPGs and the like, don't they? Thief characters. They're fast, and steal items. Well, I was never into games much. But it's not like I've never played one."

"I don't...really know, but if I can avoid panicking, those... Did you call them dream monsters? I think it's not impossible for me to fight monsters like those."

"It'll be up to your magic, I guess. If all you can manage is common dream monsters, there's a crazy guy out there you won't stand a chance against."

Was that "crazy guy" the king?

The clear surface that was not actually a lake was now completely covered in ripples.

In the smoky distance, he could vaguely make out something like a pillar that reached up to the polka dot sky.

"That's...the Iron Tower of Heaven?" he asked slowly.

"Yep. Think of it as Parano's navel. If you use the Iron Tower of Heaven as a point of reference, along with things like which direction you need to go in to get to which ruin, you can figure out relative locations that way."

Just how much longer would they have to walk to reach the Iron Tower of Heaven? He wanted to ask, but he refrained. He could more or less guess the answer on his own. In Parano, thinking about time, or how much longer something would be, was meaningless.

"So, dream monsters, they're not that common, huh?" he asked.

"It's my fault. The weak ones get scared, and run off. It's different when a star falls and everything goes wild, though."

"You're famous?" Haruhiro questioned.

Alice shrugged. "I'll bet that dream monsters can sense ego. They don't have any themselves—they can't—but they want it, so they attack people. But when an ego is too strong, it becomes threatening to the dream monsters."

"When you kill dream monsters... you can steal their ego?" Haruhiro asked.

"Id."

"You can steal that, and get stronger?"

"It's not that you'll get stronger. Your magic becomes stronger."

It seemed it was the nature of ego and id to fluctuate in order to balance each other out.

If Alice had an ego of 100, Alice's id would settle at around 100. The opposite was also true. If Alice killed a dream monster with 10 id, Alice would go up to 110 id. From there, Alice's ego would automatically get stronger until it approached 110. It wouldn't happen all at once, but grow gradually.

"If my ego were... let's say 10, would my id be 10, too?" Haruhiro asked.

"More or less, yeah."

"So if I kill a monster with 10 id, my id will become 20, and my ego will increase to 20, too."

"That would be the hope."

Alice was being evasive. Were his calculations off? No matter how he thought about it, ten plus ten was twenty, but maybe not in Parano.

When they reached the edge of the land of ripples, they came to a place with sand that could only be described as pure blue. Here and there, there were yellow, mushroom-like things with their caps spread out. Were they mushrooms?

When the two of them got closer, the yellow things were two meters across, and looked like turtles carrying mushrooms on their backs. They didn't move, and were hard as rock to the touch.

They were really bizarre, but not particularly surprising. Parano had lots of strange things. Or rather, it was full of nothing but strange things.

"I have to find my magic..." Haruhiro muttered.

"I survived because I had my shovel," Alice agreed. "Hup!"

And Alice jumped on top of one of the yellow mushrooms that was not in fact a mushroom.

"In that moment, at least, this shovel was all I could rely on. Only my shovel. One way of thinking about it is that something like that may have a possibility of becoming your magic, and..."

"...It might not?" Haruhiro finished.

"Why do you think the dream monster you gave birth to took that form?"

"That's... I wonder. I feel like I had a dream, but I hardly remember it."

"That's how it goes. Even if we're able to convince ourselves that something's the answer, it's awfully hard to find absolute proof."

In the blue sand where the yellow mushrooms that were not mushrooms were scattered around, the two of them walked, and walked, and walked.

It all seemed like a made-up story. Even when it came to events that were carved into his head and heart, the moment Haruhiro stopped being able to feel they had actually happened, they fell to pieces and slipped through the gaps in his fingers.

Without the other person known as Alice C, even if he had survived, his sense of reality would have weakened, vanished, and he might have lost all his memories.

At some point, the number of mushrooms that were not mushrooms increased to the point that they blotted out the surface, making it impossible to see the sand.

The tops of the mushrooms that were not mushrooms were slippery, making it hard to walk, but the two of them had to press onward.

Suddenly, he felt hungry. His guts were wriggling in search of food. Despite that, his stomach didn't growl.

His throat was dry. He wanted something to drink. He didn't know why, but there was a pain in the back of his eye.

"Water," Haruhiro gasped. "Something to eat…"

"Didn't I tell you this the first time? Even if you don't eat or drink, you won't die. It's been a long time since I've put anything in my mouth."

"But it's driving me crazy."

"Why not drink your own spit?"

Haruhiro decided to try that. He wasn't satisfied with that answer, but if he didn't drink something, spit or otherwise, this was going to get out of hand.

The garden of yellow mushrooms that were not mushrooms was suddenly replaced by rugged, gray rocks. The rocks had countless little horsetail-like things growing from them. They'd be edible, wouldn't they?

He plucked a few, and when he went to toss them in his mouth, he realized Alice was watching him, and stopped.

When he squeezed the small pseudo-horsetails, a golden yellow fluid came out, and it stank like it was rotten. The fact that he still felt an urge to lick it was, he had to admit, terrifying.

The rocks rose and fell, and they found them going down when they tried to climb and going up when they were trying to descend.

When he turned upwards on an impulse, there was no sky. Turning to his right, he saw the sky there. It was like he was walking on a wall, but he didn't fall.

It wasn't like that all the time. The ground formed a gentle spiral, with the sky above sometimes, below at others, sometimes to the left, and sometimes to the right.

Occasionally his hunger and thirst made a comeback. He often resented Alice for being perfectly fine with this state.

Hunger and thirst stirred up the heart. Because of that, he tried to extinguish his frustration and hatred. It worked sometimes, and didn't others.

He was finally starting to be able to see the Iron Tower of Heaven clearly.

"It's like a radio tower, isn't it?" Alice said. "Too big and too tall, though."

Alice was saying things that he felt like he understood, but maybe didn't. Regardless, the Iron Tower of Heaven, true to its name, was assembled from iron materials, and was a grand structure that seemed to reach up to the heavens.

Looking at it from the spiral hill, it wasn't just the tower itself that was iron, but the area around it, too. There were tens—no, hundreds—of ten-meter rusty iron walls surrounding the tower.

The iron walls had gates with iron bar doors. When they went through one gate, another iron wall stood in their way on the other side. They followed the wall, and there was another gate. They went through the gate, and then followed the wall again.

There was a gate. They went through it, following the wall.

This repeated for a long time.

"I remember the path, but if I didn't, we'd get lost," Alice said. "There are a lot of dead ends."

"It's practically a maze."

"That this place doesn't change is its one saving grace. If it changed every time, we'd have to go by trial and error."

Slowly but surely, he was becoming more able to cope with the hunger and thirst. In place of those discomforts, or maybe not, his longing for his comrades grew stronger and stronger.

Whenever it got to be too much, he asked Alice for permission, and then screamed his head off while rolling around.

Alice didn't say, *Are you an idiot?* or *What are you doing?* or anything like that.

When they were through the iron maze, there was a mountain of old iron scraps piled up, and on top of them, the Iron Tower of Heaven rose into the sky.

The Iron Tower of Heaven had an external set of stairs. It was just an iron frame with steps about a meter wide and no hand rail, so it would have been tough on someone with a fear of heights.

The steps were made of iron, and thin enough that they warped a little if you stepped down on them hard. The whole set of stairs shook a little, too.

When they had gone up about a hundred meters or so, the stairs stopped. There was a ladder. A long ladder. It had to be fifty meters, at a minimum.

The wind picked up, and it tasted sweet even through the mask. He was a little scared, but he somehow made it up the ladder, and then there were more stairs to climb.

He climbed stairs, climbed a ladder, climbed stairs. Climbed a ladder, climbed stairs.

Alice came to a stop at a landing on the stairs.

It was a strange landing. If one were to name this landing, it would probably be for the statue of a man, sitting with his legs over the edge of the landing.

Was this statue iron, too? Or had it been made just by packing rust together? It seemed like it could have been. That was how rusty it was.

The man was medium weight, medium height, and in his twenties or thirties. His hands were on his thighs, and he seemed to look off into the distance.

Bam! Alice whacked the statue in the head.

"When something's here too long, this happens."

"What happens?" Haruhiro asked hesitantly.

"It rusts. Yes, humans do, too."

"Then this guy was..."

"Before he rusted, he was living and breathing."

"Someone you knew?"

"He's been here whenever I've come, you know. Rusting a little at a time. I warned him he was in trouble, but he insisted it was fine, so...he got what he wished for."

The man, of course, didn't move a muscle. Was he still alive? He didn't look it. But this was Parano. It might be that even with his whole body turned to rust, he wasn't dead.

"We can't stay here long," Alice said. "If you're fine with rusting, it's another matter, though."

"It's dangerous, you mean?"

"You'll be fine if you don't stay. I've come several times, and even gone up higher, but I haven't rusted."

"Whether we're here a long time or a short one, this is Parano.

I thought time didn't matter..."

"It shouldn't, no. But the fact of the matter is, he's turned to rust, hasn't he?" Alice said, patting the man on the head. Then Alice pointed in the direction the man was looking.

The majority of the ground was covered in a milky white haze. It was like a sea of clouds. However, there were places dotted around where the terrain was exposed.

When he looked in the direction Alice was pointing, were those flowers, maybe?

There were flowers of many colors blossoming.

"That's Ruin No. 2," said Alice. "Or it used to be. Bayard Garden. I'll be going there to play next."

Alice started descending the steps they had climbed with light steps.

Before chasing after her, Haruhiro tried touching the rusted man's cheek. It was cold. The rust got on his fingers.

While he rubbed his fingers together to get the rust off, he muttered, "I will find my comrades" to himself repeatedly.

And in order to do that, he needed Alice. That was why he'd follow for now.

He was just buying time, right? He didn't really want to search, did he? He was afraid to search for his comrades, and afraid to be forced to accept the results. This was just him putting that off, wasn't it?

Besides, even if he looked around for them, he might never find a thing.

He felt his knees going weak. He nearly ended up crouching.

Alice was going down the stairs. They'd be out of sight soon.

He was struck by an urge to sit down next to the man.

Of course, he wouldn't do it.

Not for now, at least.

18 | Magic

THE VAST HILLY AREA was blanketed in flowers, flowers, and more flowers of all sizes.

That hill had red flowers blooming on it. The opposite slope had a mixture of yellow and orange flowers. There were purple flowers. There were blue flowers, too. There were white flowers, and there were pink flowers.

As for lasting traces of the ruins, there was only the debris of buildings poking up through the flowers here and there. It was mostly crumbling walls, often only pillars, covered in moss, wrapped in ivy, and having become one with the landscape.

"When it was a town, it was called Imagi, I think," Alice said. "I seem to recall hearing that name."

Alice had warned Haruhiro to make absolutely sure he didn't step on any of the flowers.

These flowers hadn't grown here on their own. They had been

gathered from all over, planted, cultivated, maintained, and put in order.

It was impossible to tell from a distance, but this garden had thin paths about fifty centimeters across running all through it. The two of them followed those paths as they progressed across the hill.

"Um... If I do step on a flower, then what?" Haruhiro asked.

"They'll get mad."

"Who will?"

"The person we're about to go see."

It was apparently called Bayard Garden, but this was Ruins No. 2, an unchanging place. The number of hills wouldn't go up or down. Or it wasn't supposed to, at least.

They crossed seven—no, eight—of those gentle, flower-covered hills. Or was it nine? More, maybe.

At first, Haruhiro was struck by the beauty of them. Now, he felt nothing.

The flowers, the hills, what did any of it matter?

"Alice," he said.

"What?"

"I don't know why, but for a while now... I'm not sure when it started... anyway, my comrade's names, they won't come to me. Their faces do, though."

"How about you think of their faces, then go through all the sounds their names could start with? A, i, u, e, o, ka, ki, ku, ke, ko, and so on."

"A, i, u, e, o..."

He went all the way to "wa, wo, and n," but nothing came to mind.

"Weird," he said. "There's no way I'd forget them."

"You can forget anything," Alice told him. "Me, I can't remember my parents' names or faces."

"I've never remembered my parents to begin with, though..."

"Oh, you mean how you don't know a thing about your life before you woke up in that Grimgar place, right? Well, it's not that weird that you'd forget your comrades' names, then."

"If I really do forget them...it'll be like they never existed in the first place."

"Shihoru. Kuzaku. Merry. Setora? Oh, and what was it again? Kiichi? Yume. Umm, also Ranta? Then Manato. Moguzo?"

Haruhiro stared at Alice. "Why do you know?"

"You told me, remember? Well, I can't guarantee they're correct, though."

"They're all right," he said slowly. "No mistakes. You got them all."

It was a good thing he'd realized he was starting to forget his comrades. The way things were going, their very existence would have vanished from his head.

Either way, they were irreplaceable, so why had he been about to forget his comrades, who meant more than anything to him?

Haruhiro meant to find them no matter what, but on the other hand, he might have wanted to forget. If he could just completely forget, that would be easier.

That's not true, he wanted to think. But that sort of desire may have been bubbling away inside him, without him ever noticing.

Of course, in Grimgar, even if he wanted to forget something, it wouldn't be easy. But in Parano, even the things that should have been unforgettable might slip away into oblivion.

"Hold on to the things that matter to you, or you'll lose them in no time," Alice told him. "In this place, a moment and an eternity are the same. But the truth is, all we ever have is 'now.' That's what it means. An eternity and an instant, they are essentially equal in value. Haruhiro. If you had known you might never meet your comrades again, if you had known that from the beginning, what would you have done?"

While they walked over the hills of flowers, a yellow bird was sitting in the middle of the narrow road. It had long feathers on top of its head. Were those called a crest? Its cheeks were round, red, and adorable.

"A parrot? Or a parakeet, maybe?" Haruhiro wondered. "What's it doing here...?"

"Suzuki-san," Alice said to the bird.

"Hey, Alice." The bird called Suzuki-san said in a voice that was a little too clear to sound like an imitation of human speech. If it were not a bird, but a middle-aged or slightly older man, it would have fit better. That was the kind of voice it was. "Come to call on our flower girl, Haname?"

"Well, yeah," said Alice. "Taking it easy here, like always, Suzuki-san?"

"It's a comfortable place." Suzuki-san chirped and occasionally cocked his head to the side as he spoke. His mouth moved too fast, and it was hard to say if it matched his vocalizations. "If you don't rub Haname the wrong way, it's lovely here."

"I'm thinking I may impose on her for a while, too."

"I see you have a newcomer in tow," Suzuki noted. "Don't go starting any trouble. I'm a pacifist, you know."

"You shouldn't get too close to me, then."

"I just wanted to say hello. You know me. I'm always a polite person." Then Suzuki-san flapped his wings, flying off somewhere else.

"Was that a half-monster?" Haruhiro asked. "Or something? It didn't seem like a dream monster. Was it a trickster, maybe?"

"Suzuki-san's a human. That's his doppel."

"A type of magic?"

"Yeah. Self-esteem, I think it's called? For those who don't have much of it, or who hate themselves, it's common for them to gain the ability to call a doppel. For people with a lot of self-love, they generally use narci, which just makes them stronger themselves. It's the most boring kind of magic. Basically, it's a projection of your consciousness, or overall disposition."

"So, Haname is..."

"She's a trickster," Alice said. "The master of Bayard Garden."

"Um, er... a trickster? We're meeting one? Now?"

"She's usually a quiet, likable person. It should be fine, I think."

Haruhiro made doubly sure to watch where he stepped. He'd

been being careful ever since Alice's original warning, but Suzuki-san had been suggesting Haname was scary when angry, so extra caution couldn't hurt.

"Personally, I'd like to go search for my comrades quickly," Haruhiro sighed.

"I won't rush. If you want to go, why not go by yourself?"

"Even if I were to act alone, honestly... I wouldn't know where to look."

"Now that you know about the Iron Tower of Heaven, you can go anywhere, and get back."

"So that's why you took me there."

"I can be kind like that sometimes, yes."

Haruhiro came to a stop. He turned back, thinking, *Maybe I should go it alone.*

If he said, *I'm going,* Alice might stop Haruhiro. Alice might come up with some reason or other, and have him keep following her. That's probably what Haruhiro was hoping for.

When had he gotten so weak? No, he had been like this all along. As a volunteer soldier trainee, he'd never done anything for himself without Manato's say-so.

If he'd gotten serious back then, doing the best he could, maybe they wouldn't have lost him?

"Alice," he called out, but not to stop the other person. "Alice C."

He already had his back to Alice. He couldn't hear any footsteps, so Alice had probably stopped.

Without turning back, Haruhiro said, "I'm going. I'll find my comrades."

"Oh, yeah?"

"Oh, and maybe my magic, too."

"Well, give it your best shot."

If they parted here, they'd never meet again. He had that feeling. It made him feel a little lonely, but there was no hesitation.

No. The reason he didn't turn, it was because he felt like it would dull his resolve. He was hesitating. He had to think he wasn't, or he couldn't go forward, so he told himself he felt no hesitation.

Haruhiro touched the mask covering his mouth. "Thanks for the mask."

"It was nothing, really."

He was about to say, *See you around,* but Haruhiro swallowed the words, and took a step forward.

If he could act on the spur of the moment, he could let that take him as far as it would.

He'd be alone from here on. Alone forever, maybe.

His chest tightened.

It was scary, but if his feet would move through the fear, he could move forward that much more. He found himself wanting to call his comrades' names. He couldn't have forgotten them again already, right?

It's fine, he reassured himself. *I know them. But hold back for now. Until I'm out of Bayard Garden, at least. How far do I have to walk? Maybe I should run.*

Even though he didn't run, he did quicken his pace a little.

It happened right after that.

There was something moving on the hill up ahead. It was

several hundred meters away, possibly more, so he couldn't see it well. But it was traveling the narrow paths.

Was it human? The first idea to come to mind was Ahiru. But it wasn't him. From the shape of it, it didn't look human. A dream monster, maybe?

With Alice so close by? The dream monsters were supposed to fear Alice. That meant it was a half-monster, a human absorbed by a dream monster, huh? That, or someone's doppel, maybe.

Haruhiro drew his dagger and readied himself.

It was—a spider. But the legs were like an octopus's. A human-octopus-spider.

Its movement was by no means slow; in fact, it was pretty fast. It had already closed to forty, fifty meters.

It was bigger than a person, and many-legged, so with skillful manipulation of those numerous octopus legs, it could race down a road that was no more than fifty centimeters across.

"Ahahahahahah! Ahahahahahahahahahah! Ahahahahah! Ahahahahahahahahahah!"

It was laughing about something, too. It had a human head, after all. Maybe it shouldn't have been surprising it could.

The voice was crazy.

"Hold on...?" Haruhiro could already make out the eyes and nose of the human-octopus-spider clearly.

That hard-looking hair. The glasses. The snub nose. The angular face. And that voice.

"Ahihihiiii! Heehah! Ehihiohohohohohoh! Gyahahahahbyo-hohogyuheheeh!"

"...Kejiman?"

"Doppoooooooooooooooooooo...!" The octopus legs retracted, then extended quickly, and the creature sprang. Kejiman did.

No, was it Kejiman? The face looked like Kejiman. Like, they were two peas in a pod. It was just like Kejiman.

The creature hadn't just jumped straight up. In other words, it wasn't a vertical leap; it was coming this way. It was jumping at him, wasn't it? If he didn't get out of the way, it was going to hit him head-on, wasn't it?

Naturally, Haruhiro wasn't empty-headed enough to sit still in a situation like this. The spot where he expected the human-octopus-spider that looked like Kejiman to land and Haruhiro's current position were one and the same, so he could avoid trouble by moving.

Instead of backing away, yeah, he was better to move up. If this were a place where he had freedom of movement, he'd have done a forward roll, but he couldn't disturb the flower garden, so he ran down the narrow path with his posture kept low.

Kejiman soared over Haruhiro's head.

No, he didn't know for sure it was Kejiman, though.

There was a weird, wet landing sound behind him. When he did an about-face, the human-octopus-spider that looked like Kejiman was turning around, and he saw Alice racing towards them from the other side.

"Hey, don't step on the flowers!" Alice shouted.

Alice probably wasn't saying that to Haruhiro, but to the human-octopus-spider that looked like Kejiman. He had to question whether it could understand what they were saying, but it was kind of too late.

Letting out a "Shaaaaaaaa..." or some other sound, the human-octopus-spider that looked like Kejiman turned in his direction. Its octopus legs were outside the walkway, cruelly trampling the pure white flowers.

"Haruharuharuharuharuharuharuhirorororororororororor ororooooooo..."

"No, man..." Haruhiro mumbled.

This thing was Kejiman. Or it had originally been Kejiman, at least.

He wanted to cry. There weren't many guys who could be this much of a nuisance, you know? Also, the way its tongue moved while going "Rorororororororororororo" was exceedingly gross.

Hold on, it was stepping on the flowers. Now what?

"How could you...!" Alice sprang at the ex-Kejiman.

The shovel had peeled, and tens of blackish belts of skin wrapped around the ex-Kejiman. It went without saying, but those things weren't just skin. They had protected Alice and Haruhiro from the whirling maelstrom of debris. They were tough, but also sharp.

Tens of those blackish belts of skin sliced the ex-Kejiman into ribbons. Even just being brushed by the belts, they easily cut through the ex-Kejiman like it was made of jelly.

"Urgh..." Haruhiro stepped back despite himself.

The ex-Kejiman's torso was like a massive spider, and the legs were like an octopus's. Kejiman's head was jutting out from the top of the torso section. The belts of skin wildly slashed not just the torso, or just the legs, but all of him without any mercy. It wouldn't be long before Kejiman's head was snipped off.

But, right before it could be...

...Kejiman slipped free.

As if he had just been launched out of the torso, a naked Kejiman went flying.

It looked kind of like Kejiman had just been born out of an octopus-spider.

"Eek! Eeeeeeeek!" Kejiman screamed.

Having fallen on the narrow path, the man was now crawling this way.

Haruhiro backed off even further. The guy was naked, after all. He was also covered all over in mucus, and was sticky and slimy. Even if he hadn't been all of those things, this wasn't a man Haruhiro ever wanted to get close to.

"Haruhirorororororo!" Kejiman wailed. "Haruhirororororoooo! Rorororororororororororororo!"

"No! Stay away!"

"That's awfully cold of youuuu..."

Kejiman stood up. The octopus-spider had already fallen to pieces, and was scattered all over.

Alice jumped over the remains, shovel at the ready. "A human came out of a dream monster? What is that guy? Haruhiro, is he a friend of yours?"

"No, he's not my friend..."

"If we ain't friends, what are weee, Haruhiro?" Kejiman whined. "Say my naaaaaaame."

"It's Kejiman, right?"

"I'm Kejimananan? Whuhwhawhawhawhawhat? Whawhawhawhawhahwahwhawhawha."

His tongue was thrust out, moving back and forth at incredible speed. Kejiman's eyes were spinning rapidly round and round in their sockets. His blood vessels were all raised, and pulsating. He was clearly not in any normal state. He was done for.

It might be heartless, but they had to finish him. Whether he was a half-monster or something else that Haruhiro didn't know, Kejiman had become some sort of monster.

But it was questionable if Haruhiro could do it. He had no confidence.

"A-Alice..."

He was sorry to do it, but he'd have to turn to Alice for help. Though, even if Haruhiro hadn't asked, the shovel in Alice's hands was already peeling.

Farewell, Kejiman, he thought. *May we never meet again. I mean, if I'd never met you in the first place, we wouldn't even be in this mess.*

"ΩΩΩΩχχχχχχχΩΩΩχχχχχχχΩΩχχχχχχχΩΩΩχχχχ χχχχχΩΩΩχχχχχχχχΩΩχχχχχχχχΩΩΩχχχχχχχΩΩχχχχ χχχχχχΩΩΩΩΩχχχχχχΩΩΩΩχχχχχχχ...!"

Haruhiro staggered. Was that a sound? It was ultrasonic, or an ultra-vibration, or something. There was a pain in his ears, but it also threw off his equilibrium, making him stumble around badly.

It wasn't just Haruhiro. The naked Kejiman was clutching its head, and even Alice was partially cowering.

Alice shouted "...name!" or something like that.

...name...

...name...

Haname, huh. The master of Bayard Garden. A trickster.

You mustn't step on the flowers in this place, Haruhiro remembered.

Kejiman had broken that taboo. He had incurred the wrath of Haname. Was this the result?

From the edge of the land, something gradually spread across the sky. It grew larger and larger, painting over the polka dot sky, expanding, occupying it. It wasn't a simple color, and it was hard to say what colors it was. The coloration changed moment to moment, and it was shining, too, almost like an aurora. However, it was clearly different from a phenomenon involving electrical discharge. It was there as a solid object.

Was it an object, or, since it was moving, was it a creature? It was so big that "huge" didn't begin to cover it. It was like a bird, or a butterfly, or a moth, or something that had its wings spread, and was trying to blot out the sky.

Could it be... that was her?

"...Haname?" Haruhiro whispered.

Nah, couldn't be. It was clearly way too big for that. It probably wasn't Haname herself, but a phenomenon being brought about by Haname's power. That was probably a better way to think of it.

Naturally, it was still amazing enough that he wanted to pray this was some sort of mistake. What was going to happen now? He couldn't imagine, but Haname, or the thing that was Haname's power, which was trying to fill the sky, appeared to be forming waves. If it were some sort of massive butterfly or moth, it might have been trying to beat its wings.

He felt a wind. It wasn't sweet. Up and up, the atmosphere was being sucked.

"Uh-oh! Uh-oh! Uh-oh! Uhoh-oh! Uhohohohoh-oh!" Kejiman was on all-fours, clinging to the ground.

"Ah!" Haruhiro's body was lifted up.

Oh, crap.

He was flying.

Hold on, they were flying away.

The flowers.

The flowers of Bayard Garden, countless petals of red, yellow, orange, purple, blue, white, and pink were being swept up.

"No! Hold on?!" Haruhiro flailed desperately, trying to return to the ground.

But he was floating.

Haruhiro was already in the air.

Maybe there was nothing he could—

"Haruhiro!" Right beneath him, Alice had the shovel thrust into the ground.

The shovel peeled, and the blackish belts of skin reached for Haruhiro. Perhaps Alice was trying to save him. But wouldn't this cut him? Was it safe?

The blackish belts of skin embraced and wrapped around Haruhiro with a surprising tenderness.

Having pulled Haruhiro down, Alice forced him to the ground.

"Kyaaaaaaaa!" Kejiman wailed. "Kyuuuuuuuu! Kyoooooooooooo...?!"

The naked Kejiman was sucked up into the sky. Hold on, why was he swimming? Well, even if he'd turned into a monster, he couldn't swim through the sky. He was just moving his arms and legs like that to give the impression of swimming.

Alice deployed the shovel's skin like a tent. In no time, tens of those skins were stuck tightly together, leaving not even the slightest gap. Alice cut off the outside from the inside, sealing it away. The violent air currents outside could blow as wildly as they wanted, but only the sound of wind reached inside.

"Here's hoping this is enough to quell her anger," Alice said. "I'm not counting on it, though."

"Don't tell me," Haruhiro gulped. "That big thing, that's Haname?"

"She's not always like that. She looks like a beautiful woman. No face, though."

"Oh... I see, so she has no face..."

"This is all because that gross thing stepped on the flowers."

"If anything, it's Haname herself who's the one messing them up..."

"When she gets mad, she loses control, but as far as tricksters go, she's one of the better ones."

One of the better ones.

That was one of the better ones?

Seriously? Tricksters were scary. He didn't want to have anything to do with them.

"Haruhiro," said Alice.

"...Yes?"

"I bet it's a mystery to you why I came all the way to Haname's place."

"Well... yeah, it is, honestly."

"Even if she's an incredibly troublesome connection, she's better than nothing," Alice said. "If you think you can get by in life without getting involved with people, you're wrong."

Suddenly, Ranta's face flashed through his mind. Even if the guy was an ass, if he were here now, it would be a little—no, very—reassuring. He'd meant to search for his comrades alone, but that resolution was already wavering.

Should he do something about this unbearable weakness, try to cast it aside somehow? Or did he have to accept his weak self, and continue to get by somehow?

When he was with his comrades, Haruhiro's role was clear, choosing goals was simple, and he just had to push towards them. When he was alone, he couldn't stick to the things he did manage to decide, and he quickly wavered.

"That's who you are, I suppose," Alice suddenly whispered. Right hand still holding the bare shovel, Alice grabbed Haruhiro by the collar with the left hand. "Get up."

"Huh?"

Obeying Alice's order, even though he was dubious about it, Haruhiro was shocked when Alice put a hand around his waist.

"...Huh? What? Why...? Huh?"

"I thought something was weird. I could feel it," Alice said. "Using magic is fairly tiring, but when I'm next to you, my body feels light somehow. Basically, my magic is stronger."

The bare shovel was flickering a faint red. If Alice took off the mask, what would Alice look like?

Maybe Alice could tell what he was thinking.

"It's okay," Alice said in a whisper. "My mask, you can take it off. You want to see, right?"

His hands trembled. They didn't hesitate. Haruhiro shifted Alice's mask down below the chin.

"I'm pretty normal," said Alice. "Disappointed?"

"...Nah."

"The search for your comrades," Alice told him. "Let me help you with it, Haruhiro. If you can help me with your magic, that is."

"My...magic?"

"There are four types of magic. I told you that, didn't I?"

"Philia, narci, doppel... I've only heard about three."

"That's because it's my first time seeing the fourth. Resonance."

"...That's what mine is?"

"Yep. The thing about resonance, it makes other people's magic stronger. That's all."

"So basically...I can't do anything on my own?"

"Perfect for you, huh," Alice said with a faint smile.

His heart had been racing for a while now. He didn't want that to get noticed. But Alice already knew for sure.

I'm not ugly, Alice had said.

That took some gall. This went well beyond not being ugly.

There was a female elf named Lilia in the party of Soma, who led the Daybreakers. Being an elf, her facial structure was fundamentally different from humans', giving her an otherworldly beauty.

If he were forced to describe it, Alice was like Lilia. Not quite comparable to other humans. The nose, the eyes, the lips... was it strange that those shapes, those sizes, was able to make him think Parano wasn't so bad, after all?

It was as if some creator god had carefully perfected Alice's face at the micron level. Like the slightest breath might make it all crumble, but it was far too valuable to destroy.

Alice had talked about being badly bullied. Whether physically or mentally, he couldn't understand what those hurting Alice had been thinking.

If it were Haruhiro, he'd likely have been too terrified to even approach. If possible, he didn't want to be anywhere close. To just see it occasionally from a distance was enough.

Was Alice actually real?

Was this a dream, after all?

Even after this, Haruhiro would go on to think that many times.

He would also think this:

If only it could all be a dream.

Grimgar of Fantasy and Ash

19 | Behold, Her Tears Are Beautiful

IT DIDN'T REALLY MAKE SENSE, but Kuzaku wasn't in bad shape. His whole body was full of energy. It was no exaggeration to say he was in peak condition.

The fact of the matter was, his muscles were pumped up, and his armor was tight. Thanks to that, though it felt a bit cramped, his body was feeling more than sharp enough to compensate for that. He'd never felt so sharp before—which was all well and good, but...

He raised his voice to call his comrade's name. "Shihoru-san!"

The voice that came out was really big, and it even surprised him. He was in a forest where the ground, the trees, and everything else was jet black, despite it not even being night, facing her down with his large katana in hand.

"Wake up already! You're not that kind of girl, Shihoru-san!"

"Whyyyy?" Shihoru wailed.

Her body was covered here and there with something that

looked like sparkling spiderwebs. Not on her clothes, on her bare flesh.

It was like he could almost see but couldn't, or almost couldn't see but could, but basically she was more or less naked.

Also, had her hair always been that long? Her lips were awfully glossy, puffy, and her eyes were sleepy, and slightly moist.

What in the world had happened to cause this? Was it like that?

All Kuzaku could say was, *Stuff happened.*

Well, not that he knew what most of that stuff was. In the end, he could use all the words he wanted; and he still wouldn't have been able to describe it.

"I'm not that kind of girl?" Shihoru cried. "I'm not what kind of girl? How can you say I'm not that kind of girl, Kuzaku-kun? Huh? How?"

"No, but...Shihoru-san, you and I are comrades! We've been together all this time! We've shared good times and bad times! But the way you look now..."

"You don't want to see?"

She started fondling her own breasts. She was gasping.

Whoa, whoa, whoa, wh-wh-what was she doing? Kuzaku nearly averted his eyes, but stopped himself.

It wasn't that he wanted to see. No? If he said he *didn't* want to see, would that be a lie? No. It wasn't about wanting to see or not.

"This is crazy, Shihoru-san!" he cried. "You're acting crazy!"

"Maybe I am. I feel like I'm going crazy."

"No, not that's not it! Damn it! We need to be searching for Haruhiro, and Merry-san, and Setora-san, and even Kiichi, but I can't even talk to you!"

"Forget talk," said Shihoru. "I don't care about that."

Out of nowhere, she started crying. But the sparkling tears that overflowed from her eyes, poring out, were not liquid. In fact, the spiderweb-like material covering her naked body... it was her tears.

The way she looked as she cried was strikingly beautiful, but he couldn't afford to just keep looking.

The tears overflowed without end, wrapping around her, like diamond accessories, perhaps making her even more beautiful. In addition, they ran down her legs as they glittered, pooling at her feet.

"What's going on, seriously?!" Kuzaku lowered his hips, large katana at the ready.

His body was moving really well. How many of those weird monsters had he killed on the way here?

The more he killed, the more muscle he built, and the sharper his skills as a swordsman became. His muscles became healthier, tougher, making Kuzaku stronger in a straightforward manner. The way things were going, he'd live to three hundred. Thanks to that, he was able to cut down one monster that attacked after another.

"The truth is, I don't care." While crying, Shihoru raised her right arm. In time with her motion, the spiderweb-like stuff pooled at her feet, her jewel-like tears, danced towards Kuzaku. Those tears were bad news.

"Grrrrrr...!" Kuzaku swung with all his might. No matter what he did, he couldn't cut through her tears. And so he swung his large katana, pushing them away with the wind.

When her tears were scattered by his sword pressure, they hit the black ground and trees nearby, those parts sparkled brightly, and they were plainly crushed.

Was that possible? Really? It was scary. What was going on there? Kuzaku had no idea.

"What happened to you, Shihoru-san?!" he yelled.

She was still crying in anguish, and her brutal tears were pressing towards him.

Kuzaku backed away one step, then two as he swung, blocking the tears at the last moment, but it was weird that he could block them at all.

This power, it was kind of not normal, wasn't it?

Is this some sort of nightmare? he wondered repeatedly.

All jokes aside, he wanted this to be a dream.

Grimgar
of
Fantasy and Ash

Now then, *Grimgar of Fantasy and Ash* is on its 13th volume now.

Writing it, there were times I went, *Oh, I see, so that's what's going to happen,* but I wonder how the next one will turn out.

That's one thing I just can't know until I write it. I'm hoping what happens afterwards isn't too terrible, because no matter what it is, I'm the one who has to write it, after all.

By the way, there was a special version of this book with a drama CD that released at the same time, and I wrote the script for it.

From the beginning, I wanted to have Director Ryosuke Nakamura of the *Grimgar of Fantasy and Ash* anime be the audio director for it, so I made it a story that took both the anime and novel into consideration.

Director Nakamura's Grimgar really distilled the essence of Grimgar, and I felt, "This is Grimgar," watching it, but there were also parts that were different from my Grimgar.

Director Nakamura has the sense, technique, and talent that I lack, and he portrayed a Grimgar I couldn't have in the anime.

I wanted to try writing a script that took advantage of that, and I personally had a great desire to hear a drama CD directed by Director Nakamura and featuring the cast of the anime.

While writing this afterword, I've yet to hear the final product, but I was able to be there for the recording, so I have a vision of what it will sound like. Without a doubt, it will be something incredible. The members of the cast were really enjoying their acting, and they told me the script was good.

I think they weren't just being polite, probably. If you're interested, please listen to it. For fans of the anime in particular, you'll be missing out if you don't.

Ever since getting involved in production of the anime, I've had more opportunities to work together with many people to create something together. I like the work of a novelist, in which I can create a nearly complete work all by myself, but this showed me once again how I have only been able to continue doing that because of the support of a variety of people.

These days where, by borrowing the power of others, I can climb mountains I couldn't have otherwise, and see new vistas, are highly stimulating.

I think I will be able to use this experience in my main profession as an author, so look forward to the next volume, when Haruhiro and the others go wild... or maybe don't... in the other world.

To my editor, Harada-san, to Eiri Shirai-san, to the designers of KOMEWORKS among others, to everyone involved in production and sales of this book, and finally to all of you people now holding this book, I offer my heartfelt appreciation and all of my love. Now, I lay down my pen for today.

I hope we will meet again.

—Ao Jyumonji

Grimgar of Fantasy and Ash

Experience these great light **novel** titles from Seven Seas Entertainment

See the complete Seven Seas novel collection at
sevenseaslightnovel.com

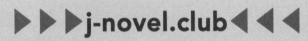